When two vacationers are reported missing in a sailing accident at a Mediterranean island, their four friends back in London decide to investigate.

Questions begin with the fact that there were originally three vacationers—Reynard, Klara and Anton. So which two are missing? Was it a tragic drowning or something sinister?

As told by the unnamed fourth member of the investigative expedition, this is a light-hearted and amorous odyssey featuring friends Roderick, Greta, and Diane as they go in search of answers. Each has theories about what happened, drawn from past romantic attachments with the missing and fond reminiscing.

Their voyage of discovery leads to island exploration and a climactic bacchanal in an old fortress. Could jealousy be a motive in the disappearance, as Roderick suspects? Has Anton, the youthful initiate into romance, rejected the advances of his two more experienced companions? Or does the island have still more to reveal?

A Passion Worth Pursuing
Copyright © 2021 A.L. Means
ISBN: 978-1-4874-3141-9
Cover art by Martine Jardin

Published by eXtasy Books Inc or
Devine Destinies, an imprint of eXtasy Books Inc

Look for us online at:
www.eXtasybooks.com or www.devinedestinies.com

A Passion Worth Pursuing

By

A.L. Means

DEDICATION

To Youth and Reflection

CHAPTER ONE

The first we heard about it was through a news agency. A reporter phoned to check details. Names, ages, addresses, that sort of thing.

Those of us who considered ourselves their friends were stunned. We were still getting over the reports of their being missing, and now this.

"Can it be true?" Greta was on the phone almost as soon as I'd finished talking to the reporter. It was good to hear her voice again, even in these circumstances. Since she'd moved back home to Denmark, I'd hankered at times for the calmness she seemed to bring to life and, let's face it, those riveting sapphire eyes.

"It's all vague," I told her. "They still haven't identified bodies. I'm not yet convinced they've found them. "

"But just two," she said with rare agitation. "And which two? You think they'll find the other one?"

"Sooner or later, I expect. I mean, bodies, supposing they've found any, can't have been far away from the boat, and that part of the Mediterranean is pretty well traveled, I think."

It was still early in the morning by my standards. I made myself the usual breakfast—cereal, toast, coffee—and reflected on the excitement we'd all felt at this very table when they announced their plans.

Reynard had put his arms around the other two, Klara and Anton—I remember that—and of course, typically enough, we grouped around in a half circle in anticipation of what he

1

might say. He had that effect. He was the pivot of our social circle, no doubt about it.

What the others expected I can't say. Perhaps it was going to be one of his ideas about living arrangements. That was my first thought. Reynard was very persuasive. People agreed to do things for him, with him, that in all probability would be rejected with scorn coming from someone else.

He was a bit of a user in that way. *Do the deed and then move on* was his unspoken dictum. But those who . . . what can I say . . . acceded to his wishes didn't seem to hold a grudge for long. Perhaps they—we—were convinced by the way he talked about "life experiences." They were a sort of hobby of his. It was as if they were collectibles, and the point of living was to assemble a set of them.

The three of them had been sharing a flat in London for several months at the time of Reynard's announcement. The precise nature of their relationship was never stated. Not that anyone considered it a taboo arrangement. It was more that Reynard took pleasure in letting us guess the details, and of course that made it the subject of endless speculation. Non-judgmental, of course.

Besides, I think we all agreed our lives would be duller without the guesswork. Reynard's trysts had been going on, and off and on again, for years.

For that matter, Reynard's relationships, in one version, had once included Greta, and in her case, it had been considerably more than friendship. When I first met her, she was an au pair, minding the children in a house overlooking the Thames in an opulent suburb. Quite how she encountered Reynard I can't say, but he glommed onto that sleek figure and those onion-skin blonde tresses with all the predatory zeal for which he was known.

Now that I think about it, I recall one of their first dates. As already indicated, he was never one to disguise his intentions when it came to intimacy, which made his successes all the more impressive. Several of us had gone to a production of *Hamlet* at a then-fashionable theatre in the round, and Reynard—under the spell of an intriguingly X-rated portrayal of Ophelia by a pop star of the era—persuaded Greta to drink too much afterward.

Back at my place—on that very same sofa I still have, over there by the fake fireplace—she nestled into his lap in that matter-of-fact way she had and they began to kiss and fondle each other with a passion to put even Ophelia to shame.

With a mixture of envy and lust we watched them blossom into nakedness, and his groans and her whinnies were almost enough to prompt us into physical activities of our own. Instead we just gloated, anticipating that this was *act one, scene one* and that someday soon all of us would have at least walk-on parts.

No surprise then when Reynard proclaimed several days later that they were engaged. And hardly more surprise when he followed up with an addendum a couple of months later to the effect that they no longer were.

There was a fatalism in his romantic affairs that one couldn't help suspecting was partly a matter of convenience. He made his conquests with the most earnest exaltations, but the bloom on the rose, once picked, usually soon faded.

It was part of his bewildering charm that mostly he was able to get away with it. Greta, as placid and absorbent as an alpine lake, downgraded from fiancée to friend with nary a complaint—that I ever heard, anyway.

So, given the twists in our friends' history, I needed time to evaluate the reporter's tale of mystery on the high seas. Was this just one more drama that would turn out to be a false alarm? Reynard alone had the wits of a cornered cat, and Klara's confidence was usually enough to see her past any threat. As for Anton, he was a retiring soul, but not an incapable one. The idea that two of them, or perhaps all three, had died in some marine disaster was hard to accept. So I was inclined to believe there was more to the circumstances than we knew. But how to find out more, that was the question.

Predictably, as we digested the news of their disappearance, Roderick took on the leadership role. He had grown up with Reynard in the same gilded suburb in which I'd first encountered them. Whether the rivalry had always been there I can't say. Nor can I say whether it was a leftover from the physical attraction they had reputedly once had for each other. Any erotic dimension was passé, in any case, by the time I knew them. The closeness was still there, though. Behind their backs we'd sometimes refer to them as "the two Rs," but woe betide you if they overheard. You didn't make fun of either of them lightly.

"We should all get together and decide what to do," Roderick said when he and I met over a drink. "Your flat, don't you think? See if Greta will come over from Copenhagen or wherever. Bet she will. And I'll contact Diane. She still carries a torch for Klara. Perhaps we should go out there and investigate."

"We don't even know exactly where the boat was found," I objected, "let alone what the story is with their bodies."

"All the more reason . . ."

There was a strain of unsavory, adventure-seeking ardor in Roderick's attitude, almost as if he was anticipating what Reynard might do in the circumstances and was trying to top it. To me this seemed inappropriate, and I tried to dilute it.

"This is all very gruesome and distressing," I said. "We have little more than rumors to go on. Their deaths could be greatly exaggerated. Knowing Reynard, there's more to it than we realize."

I did agree, however, to a meeting. We'd summon, or at least invite, members of the old clique past and present and see what we should — and what we could — do. Whether we were prepared to do something drastic, like charter a boat and go after them, remained to be seen. One thing even I conceded—we couldn't do nothing. They were, after all, our friends.

CHAPTER TWO

The thought in my mind at that time, loath as I was to express it, was that one of them had done in the other two. No doubt a ridiculous notion, but that's the thing with unraveling mysteries: nothing seems too ridiculous to consider. Anyway, I knew Roderick well enough to suspect there'd be a cynical element in his theorizing. Greta and Diane I wasn't so sure about.

If there was a culprit, the obvious candidate would be Reynard. There was a darkness at his core that must have been genetic, because there was nothing in his immediate circumstances that would warrant it. Hence his philosophy that every intense erotic affair was doomed, his and anyone else's. It was as if a love life was a graph of diminishing returns, and all anyone could do was enjoy while it lasted, then lament and move on. I remember Anton, when they were in the spring of their relationship, protesting.

"How can you believe it's predestined like that?" he asked Reynard, who responded with a condescending stare. "It's like you think it's in the hands of the gods or something."

I was afraid it wouldn't be beyond Reynard to see some chilling correlation between death and the end of a relationship. Why Anton and Klara would warrant murder after the three of them had been together all these years was another question. But it didn't take a genius to suggest at least one motive.

"Jealousy," Roderick told me during a phone call about our upcoming meeting. "Trios are always vulnerable. It's part of the attraction. Static electricity on a high wire. There's a touch of S and M there, for sure."

"So it occurred to you too then?" I said.

"It has to be a possibility, doesn't it? I mean, remember the big announcement when we were all in your flat. He made it sound then as if this expedition was make or break time for them. Perhaps things got out of hand and there was a falling out."

"Well, let's keep this to ourselves, shall we," I told him, basing my caution on Roderick's preliminary approaches to our erstwhile companions. "Diane has grown so sensitive, by the sound of it. As it was, she was a little upset that Klara would go off on this voyage without her, wasn't she?"

Back — well, it seems positively prehistoric now — let's just say long ago, there was whispered teasing about Diane being Klara's Anton. Our little clique had a tacitly acknowledged family tree, with Reynard and Klara being the root and the rest of us being the branches, not to mention various twigs that had fallen off in the breeze.

Still, that binary root was strong and enduring, no doubt about it. Reynard and Klara must have been pretty intense with each other for a while. Marriage was a possibility, so I heard, although whether Reynard could have stayed that course for long is questionable.

Fortunately for the flexibility of their relationship, Klara was as open to sexual experimentation as he was. That was a time in their lives, don't forget, when many young people were eager to redefine what was appropriate. It was all the more radical because of preceding years of conformity. "Gender is not an absolute," Reynard was fond of saying. "We're all sort of a blend, with the proportions varying between individuals."

In those early days there was a succession of shared boyfriends. Reynard would zero in on someone, mostly younger than he by some years and in some way naïve. He always had a penchant for Scandinavians, perhaps because of their supposed liberality about matters of the flesh.

In time, Klara would assert her own charms on the new finding, and sometimes there would be a bit of a tussle for possession. That was what happened when Reynard found Anton, and the speculation was that Klara found Diane to compensate.

Not that Diane wasn't quite a catch in her own right. She had that mixture of innocence and arrogance that can characterize attractive girls in their late teens. It's as if they're just catching on to the powerful effect they can have and they haven't yet figured out what to do about it.

Anyway, Diane certainly had it. There was a stony introversion to her that was accentuated by long feathery hair dangling like stalactites around alabaster cheeks and pale gray eyes. Hard to ignore for those who had a fondness for such features.

It would be intriguing to see how time had altered her, as it inevitably does even for pinups. Would there still be a semblance of the Diane I remembered from times when we were more closely involved with each other? A few days later, when she arrived at the flat for our meeting, I half-expected her to be wearing the kind of loin-cloth sized skirts and high boots in which she used to parade along the King's Road, a few years ago now.

Back then, she was one of those would-be models who worked in an office or attended college weekdays and took the Tube into Chelsea on Saturdays in the hope of media discovery or, if not that, perhaps a passing flirtation with a minor celebrity.

Once, she caught the eye of a tabloid photographer. For those of us who considered ourselves friends or at least passing acquaintances, her fleeting fame on that occasion seemed contagious. It was like touching the hem of royalty to see her there, slinky and precocious, in black and white on page three. Oh well, most of us have to move on from such exultance.

Whether such memories lingered in Diane's own mind as she perched on the edge of my sofa nursing a latte I doubt. She always struck me as a woman who lived in the moment. For that matter, she was capable of making her presence felt in any moment she so chose. So perhaps she didn't feel the need to dwell on embers of adulation. Her youthful features and trim figure still stood her in good stead.

"I thought this was a bad idea, them going off like that," she said, impatiently fiddling with jewelry and anything else within reach. She sounded like a shop assistant who'd just been denied a lunch break. At least her dress sense had been upgraded to a business casual look appropriate for her transition towards maturity. Even her cockney, with its dropped consonants, had toned down a little since the old days, when she'd crossed tongues with Klara's private school poshness.

Greta had just walked in after the usual transportation smorgasbord from the airport. It fell to me to greet her—not that it was a hardship. If there were signs of aging, I wasn't aware of them at that moment. The blue of her eyes and the delicate pink lip gloss—a new addition—had me mesmerized. The hug I gave her might have felt a bit overdone to her, but I honestly couldn't restrain myself. As the cliché has it, our reunion was like old times. Well, except for the missing trio.

Roderick's greeting was a little more reserved, as I anticipated. Back when his rivalry with Reynard was at its most intense, he'd had a brief fling with Greta. Reynard's engagement to her was off the boil by that time anyway, but Reynard still liked to be consulted about sex that might be considered a conflict of interests. Even in the liberalism of those times it had been a bit embarrassing, and ever since there'd been a strained undercurrent in exchanges between the former transgressors.

Greta had hardly entered the room before she made her contribution to the discussion.

"We owe it to them, as well as ourselves, to find out what happened."

She spoke in quiet measured statements with a slight rise in pitch at the end of sentences, as if putting a motion forward for a vote.

"Definitely," Roderick agreed, giving the word the force of a hammer confirming that motion. "It's like losing family. We have a right to know."

Then the conversation diverted for a while into more mundane topics, like jobs and home lives. It turned out none of us were inextricably involved in romance at that point, which was convenient, considering what was to follow.

As you might imagine, it took a while for the old camaraderie to be rekindled. When you haven't touched someone in a time, someone you used to have no hesitation in touching when and where you wanted, there's a form of awkwardness that doesn't exist among strangers. You wonder what's appropriate versus what might appear to be suggestive or needy even though you don't mean it to be. Or perhaps you do mean it to be.

Even so, it was amazing how quickly we re-adjusted to each other's presence. Over the next few days, as we worked out what to do and made the necessary travel arrangements, old bonds were renewed. It was almost as if we'd never drifted apart and we were back in one of those communal houses that Reynard used to rent. Once again we shared likes and dislikes, revealed confidences and dilemmas of the most intimate kind.

Not all of it was warm and fuzzy of course. Greta's penchant for order and cleanliness rubbed Roderick the wrong way after he left coffee stains and toast crumbs on the kitchen table at breakfast.

"I'd forgotten the stoic mother side of her," Roderick said after Greta had gone out for groceries. "I should have remembered she'd be trying to whip us into shape."

"You wish," I said.

"That's true; I'd still bare my bottom for her any day of the week." Roderick had lost none of his brashness, especially when Greta was not present to hear. I wondered whether his jeans still fell floorward as easily as in the past. He had been very proud of his genitals, clearly regarding size as equivalent to entitlement. They had their attractions, I had to admit. "Oh, you're so penis-centric," Diane used to tell him. But then, he's not alone in that.

"There are other ways of getting off, you know," she'd go on, mostly in retaliation when he teased her about "going over to the dark side" of all-female sex.

After a pause, just long enough to change the focus of his ardor, Roderick continued: "Diane's really looking hot, isn't she? She's gone to the gym now. She goes every morning, or at least I think she does. Not that I'm up that early."

"She's in great shape," I agreed, contemplating our cramped sleeping arrangements. Given the narrow space between them, I suspected Roderick was more aware of Diane's morning movements than he indicated. Greta had been assigned my bedroom, having come the furthest. I had moved into my closet-sized spare, and Diane and Roderick were making do with screened-off furniture—namely an air mattress for her and a couch for him. Of course the latter two could have returned to their own homes at night, but that would have detracted from the urgency of planning.

"Funny," Roderick continued, plainly unwilling to drop the subject and with his voice incorporating a little affected melodrama, "I always thought of Diane as sort of statue-like.

I can't imagine her breaking into a sweat. Well, not back then I couldn't. Butter wouldn't melt, as they say, although I dare say other substances might.

"Her and Klara used to be in that big double bed Reynard had upstairs, and I'd see them sometimes on a Sunday morning wrapped together like they'd just been lifted out of a Renaissance painting. Diane's bleached blondeness and Klara's russet tresses interlaced on the pillow. Very appealing it was."

"I don't think you should be telling me this." It was a mock protest on my part. The vision of the two women in mid embrace was too vivid to resist, and Roderick evidently saw no harm in it.

"Why not? It wasn't as if anyone was hiding anything. I wish I'd have climbed in with them, but I didn't quite have the nerve. I think Reynard did, though."

I actually was more familiar with that vision than I ever admitted to Roderick. One time I did barge in on Klara and Diane sharing that pillow, and Klara insisted that I should join them. The two of them were soft warm bookends, with me as naked as they were.

There was an exhilarating symmetry to it, with first one set of nails careening across my stomach and pelvis and then the other, the only difference being in the firmness of the touch. Where Klara's gyrations were calculated to tease—and, oh, didn't they—Diane's fingers explored this new territory tentatively. Encouraged by her mentor, however, Diane began to giggle and kiss me on my neck and cheek. I can still feel her gentle breath and their hair tickling my shoulders.

In my place, however, Roderick might have been disappointed. For the experience was not deeply carnal. The joint passing between us took care of that.

CHAPTER THREE

It was extraordinary how little news filtered back to us from the classical world in which our dearly departed friends had, well, departed. You'd think there would have been police reports and possibly even consular enquiries.

"It was an island somewhere, where it happened, wasn't it?" Roderick said. "So perhaps that explains it."

"Even islands have phones," I replied, vaguely hoping to impress Greta and Diane with my knowledge of the fringes of European civilization.

I caught Roderick's gaze alighting on Diane's modest but beautifully toned and sculpted cleavage. He leaned against the door frame as he spoke, causing his tee shirt to cling to his ribs and his jeans to undergo a similar stretch. He had his way of impressing; I had mine.

Besides, ribs were very important to all of us. Reynard had made something of an icon out of them. Nothing was more emphasized in his epistles about what made life worth living than skinniness. A show of protruding bones on the upper torso or the pelvic regions, whether male or female, made his day. Naturally, we all wished to oblige, and embraced his dictums as our own. Well, youth does relish its innocence. Who knew, back then, that flesh trumps figure in the end.

"We should book flights and leave as soon as possible. That's the only way to find out what's going on," said the methodical one among us who, of course, was Greta.

"Can't," came a firm voice from Diane.

"What do you mean *can't?*" Roderick asked.

"Can't fly." Her tone was as brittle as an obstreperous schoolgirl's. I'd never really decided whether she was being defiant when she talked like that or just plain scared. It seemed to sway Roderick, though.

"You mean you have a phobia?" he asked.

"I mean I'm shit scared. It's bad enough on a train. But taking off in a plane . . . I can't do it."

"What about a ship?" Roderick suggested.

"I might be able to do that," Diane conceded. "After a few drinks."

"Well, that can be arranged," Roderick went on. "Get loaded and you won't notice a thing."

Whether she picked up on it I don't know, but I sensed that Roderick had more than Diane's wellbeing in mind as he made the remark. I could almost see the image floating above his head in one of those comic book bubbles, Diane collapsed in his arms in a state of intoxicated undress, oblivious to his explorations. A momentary lapse into lust on his part, no doubt.

Greta looked glum at the prospect of a prolonged sea voyage rather than a cross-continent flight. But Roderick pointed out that it could, in fact, offer advantages. Perhaps we could sail direct to our destination rather than having to fly and then probably book a hotel, and then next day take a train or bus to some port or other, and finally a ferry of some kind, perhaps a very questionable kind. Who knew what the schedule would be? Trains might go one day, ferries a week later.

A ship from point A to point B might be rather exhilarating, he added, and might also give us a bit more time to consider our course of action when we arrived. Given Diane's fear of flying, we didn't have a whole lot of choices.

So it was then that the four of us found ourselves packed and stretching our sea legs on a south coast quayside, staring up at the funnels of a cruise ship bound for sundry ports in the far reaches of the Mediterranean.

The travel arrangements had been left up to Roderick—Greta having had to return to Copenhagen briefly to complete some business transactions. None of us should have been surprised, therefore, to discover that the said arrangements were arranged very much according to Roderick's personal whims. He'd booked two adjacent cabins—one, he announced, for Diane and himself and one for Greta and me.

"It is a cruise with a romantic theme, after all," he had told us as we stared at him in incomprehension when we got together at the flat to plan our departure. "We have to keep up appearances and try to fit in."

A feigned blankness rebuffed our questions about the suitability of a cruise ship of any kind whatsoever. Weren't there ferries, tramp steamers, or anything else with buoyancy that might get us there quicker and more appropriately?

What exactly Diane and Roderick would do in their cabin when it came to bedtime was their own affair. Greta and I turned out to be well-suited roommates, not ostentatious about revealing naked flesh but at the same time not self-conscious about it either. I could well imagine how those blue eyes had affected Reynard when they first met. Anything that attractive was an instant challenge to him. He was like a fox after a rodent in long grass—on sensual high alert until he had the prize in his clasp.

Once the ship got underway, there was of course a bustling social agenda. If you've ever been on a cruise, you will know how easily one can find oneself on a seesaw between maximum food intake and frenetic releases of energy. Mealtimes extend beyond the artistry of the platter—awe inspiring in itself—to lavish table decorations, dramatic presentations by wait staff, entertainment spectacles and even outlandish dress requirements. After a thorough gorging, one is then expected to fling oneself around the dance floor or risk one's dignity in some get-to-know-your-fellow-passengers game or other. Needless to say, both the food and the dignity are washed down with tidal waves of wine, beer, and suggestively named cocktails.

On the first evening, the four of us sat around a gleaming white tablecloth in a semi-circle, staring at and past two couples of about our own age. We exchanged smiles with them as a formality, and then talked among ourselves.

I think I was the first to say much.

"This isn't helping us figure out anything." As I spoke, I sipped my reef plunger, a concoction recommended by the sommelier. "I just feel more confused than ever. We should have just taken a train."

The response was mostly predictable. Greta, I was sure, felt the way I did. Roderick would have to defend his decision to opt for this mode of travel. Diane was the one who had yet to reveal her hand. For a few seconds my mind dwelt on visions of Roderick and her in their cabin. Perhaps that already had a bearing on her view of things, although sharing one of those narrow bunk beds for very long would tax the amorous designs of even the closest friends.

"What you don't know," said Roderick, piped music and general bustle making it a little hard to hear him, "What you don't know is there's a reason why I booked us on this."

"What do you mean?" Greta asked.

"*They* were on this ship," he announced. "Not the whole cruise. They flew out from home, as we know. But then they picked up the ship on the mainland, took it as far as one of the islands and, I suppose, hired their sailboat from there."

"How do you know all this?" Greta was visibly shaken, a sight I had only seen before under the most extreme combinations of sex and drugs.

"I found an itinerary at their house," Roderick said,

keeping his cool in the face of astonishment from the rest of us.

"You broke into their house?" Greta asked.

"I didn't break in. Reynard gave me a key ages ago. I was just looking around—for clues."

He waited for our reaction, which was a blend of curiosity and mild outrage, and then he continued to explain.

"I just thought, if we were on this ship, there might be some crew members who remembered something about them, and maybe we could get friendly and see what we could find out."

"Let me get this straight," I said. "You want us—some of us anyway—to become pals with some sailors and then seduce them."

"Well, that's putting it a bit more bluntly than I was thinking," Roderick admitted. "But that's the gist of it, I suppose. Doesn't mean it has to lead to sex—unless it's what you want, of course."

"And what do you suppose they might be able to tell us?" Greta asked. Judging by her stony expression, the *sex* part of it wasn't the impediment. It was more a question of whether any crew members had anything helpful to say. Even Roderick seemed to have doubts.

"I don't know, really. Something that was said. How they acted toward one another. Any disagreements they had. That sort of thing. You got to admit, Klara in particular would be hard to forget."

No objections were raised to that. It was a fair bet that we were sharing a mental picture of Klara as we last saw her, waving back to us on the far side of the passport checkers at Heathrow, her nails with an amethyst sheen and her hair dangling like copper tinsel.

It was Diane who diverted the conversation from the dead end it seemed to be heading toward. Given her onetime devotion to Klara—onetime and, for all I knew, continuing devotion—I half expected her to be squeamish about digging up info from crew members. But not a bit of it.

"I'm for giving it a go," she said.

"We might not like what we discover," I said.

"Like she slept with the captain or something?" Diane countered. "So what if she did? She always aimed high. Besides, we don't have much else to go on."

Roderick took heart.

"That's what I was thinking. Anything that sheds light. They may have hooked up with someone or talked about their plans. Who knows? In fact, knowing Reynard, it's almost a given he made an impression on someone."

Roderick's smirk as he slurred the last three words begged for a retort.

"Physical or mental, are you thinking?" I asked, and Roderick seemed obliged for the chance to complete the thought.

"A bit of both, I expect," he said with a chortle.

Whether seduction was strictly necessary in the pursuit of information was a moot point. Diane turned out to be surprisingly up for the challenge, however.

Despite her shorter hair and rather more assertive manner, I still had not adjusted to the fact that a length of time had passed since she was Klara's trophy girl. A picture of passivity she'd seemed to be then. But perhaps she had never been quite as pliant as Klara projected. Young women do sometimes have that way of appearing to be what others desire them to be.

Greta, rather out of character, suggested that Diane might add an extra layer of intrigue if she pretended to be estranged from a fictitious husband. Apparently, young merchant marine officers respond to the ambiguity of a wife who may not be a wife for long. "Available and yet attached" is how Greta described it. How she had come to that conclusion I didn't ask. It was so out of kilter with her customary straightforwardness.

Anyway, Greta sorted through her jewelry box until she found a gold band and a passable engagement ring that fitted, and Diane was ordained into a rather tenuous version of matrimony.

Of course, the adjustment in her status meant she'd also have to make adjustments in her bunking arrangements. Even maritime officers might not respond to the enticements of an estranged wife who was sharing a cabin with another man. At least that was Roderick's opinion, and it was plausible enough for Greta to reluctantly change quarters with Diane, and for me to agree to make myself scarce if it looked like the deck was about to be cleared for action. My heart wasn't entirely in it though. The disappearing act part of it, that is.

"What's wrong with a little voyeurism?" I complained. "I need a little entertainment too."

Apparently the gods sympathized, if not my fellow passengers.

"This better be worth it," Greta was heard to murmur, although Roderick didn't look too put out.

As it turned out, it was. Worth it, that is. Depending, I suppose, on how you look at it.

My view of it was particularly intimate for the simple reason that it happened a few feet in front of my half-closed eyes. Just happened to be in the wrong place at the wrong time, didn't I? I apologized later, thinking of course quite the opposite.

But I'm getting ahead of myself. Let's start with the lead up, which was as promising as it was calculated.

Formal wear was a big deal for dinner on our second night. The voyage seemed to be progressing nicely. Don't ask me what our GPS position was. We were at sea. That's all I can tell you. Distant lights and nebulous protrusions indicated a coastline, when any of us had a mind to peer through a porthole. It was like another world out there, as remote as the constellations above.

The engine was a distant and constant drone, more mantra than annoyance, and the gentle rocking from the waves lulled us into torpor long before we got to the wine. By the time passengers and crew entered the spacious dining room which was the heart of the cruising experience, everyone's attention seemed to be more on hemlines and what was under them.

Diane had spent the latter part of the afternoon perfecting her look, which emphasized fabrics that threatened to float off her willowy figure at any moment. Make-up, especially around the eyes, was calculated to revive the aura of virginal withdrawal that Klara had nurtured so effectively back when Diane first entered our social circle. It was still a tease all these years later. Jewelry was modest, befitting — or so we thought — a woman scorned. Or a wife, at least.

Greta looked equally stunning in a more inviting way, as if a handsome young officer had only to ask permission and she would have nodded approval as his fingers reached for those buttons between her breasts. I must say, had I been a young mariner or even an ancient one, those eyes of hers would have been enough to have me brushing aside albatrosses and any other obstacle to action.

Sure enough, as feed time morphed into dance floor debauchery, available males began to eye the bait. For that matter, Diane and Greta clearly appealed to the not-so-available males, too. This included a couple of the ship's junior officers, who apparently were only not-so-available until they were off duty sometime in the wee hours. Then they became very much available and proved the point with several rounds from the bar and whispered invitations to explore sections of the lower decks revealed only to the most discerning and sensitive, not to say light-headed, of females.

Occasionally, Greta or Diane would sway from the bar to

the ladies' room, detouring to the table where Roderick and I were sitting to update us. The pre-arrangement was for Roderick and me to be unobtrusive. Diane and Greta would do the hard work of encouraging disclosure while the two of us only stepped in to influence affairs when necessary. Quite what this necessity would be we hadn't determined.

"Emilio, the one I'm with, remembers Klara for sure," Diane told us during one of these sorties. "But he's playing hard to get. Don't you just hate that?"

"Well, how do you find out more?" Roderick asked in one of his blanker moments.

"How do you think?"

"Oh, that," muttered Roderick, faced with a derisive raising of eyebrows. Even Diane had her standards, which made me think that the first night in Roderick's cabin hadn't progressed quite to the extent I had imagined. Still, Roderick seemed to be of the opinion that Diane's feigned seduction would be of little consequence if it led to revelations about our three friends and their states of mind as they journeyed toward their final destination. Or, as we understood it, the final destination of two of them at least.

"You'll have to tag along," Diane said during her next sojourn at our table. She fixed me with a stare that would have scared the bravest suitor into submission.

"Tag along where, and with whom?" I gasped.

"The cabin. Emilio says he wants to escort me to my quarters. But I have an idea he wants more than a goodnight kiss. And the trouble is he's still not putting out much. Just like a man, isn't it? All talk and not much . . ."

"Indication of intent?" Roderick suggested.

"Yeah, that. Anyway," Diane continued, turning once more to me, "you better sneak into the cabin ahead of us and pretend you're asleep. Then perhaps he'll call it a night."

"So has he told you anything more?" Roderick asked.

"Well, he remembers Klara dancing with some man. But he's a bit vague on who it was, let alone what he looked like. Klara, on the other hand, he can describe right down to the heels."

Once again, images of Klara came to mind. Boots were all the rage when our group began to meld, and I can still see the arch in her step and the leather as tight as skin as she sauntered around in a lazy goose step. How she ever got them off when she undressed I'll never know, but she did. Several witnesses would swear to that.

In the minutes available to me in our cabin before Diane and her beau entered, I tried to arrange things to be as inhibiting as a berth, gently pitching and tossing in a mild sea, could be.

All I could see through the porthole was a dense and dark blue. I felt detached from the world, as if the ship were in a bottle that had been shaken until its shape was obliterated by imitation snow or sand or some such substance. I had drunk too much. We all had. I wondered if the others still remembered what we were doing here, what the point of it was. I'm not sure I did.

I chose the couch to be my resting place, figuring that it would be the first thing they'd see when the door opened. The sight of me cocooned in a blanket, with a wall light throwing shadows across the lower bunk and possibly a salvo of half-awake snores, would surely be enough to turn back a crew member still sober enough to worry about decorum.

A half hour passed, and I began to feel like an actor whose fellow thespians had failed to make their entries on stage. I tiptoed to the porthole to steal another glance into the void, then dashed back to the couch in case I got caught out of position. I coughed and spluttered and cleared my throat; in case they were in the passageway groping each other.

When Diane finally walked in, it seemed an anti-climax.

She was leading him by the hand.

Okay, I thought, let's get this over with. Now all she'll have to say is, "Oh dear, looks like we're not alone. We'll have to call it a night, I'm afraid." Then an affectionate hug in the doorway, and perhaps a little tongue-on-tongue contact, then bid him farewell and we can all get some sleep.

Almost immediately, though, I realized Diane's détente was not going to go according to plan. A goodnight peck on the cheek was no more on her mind than on his.

There was a detachment about her, almost to the point of callousness. It was a bit of a shock to me to see it. She'd been so compliant when she'd been Klara's toy. We'd all changed of course, but there are things about people—characteristics and such—that are hard to put out of your mind. Yet here she was acting like a predator, distant look in her eyes and determined grip on his arm as she led him to the bunk. It was almost as if she was about to embark on a revenge fuck, although revenge upon whom was not entirely clear to me. Perhaps it was not so much revenge as an attempt at imitation. As we tracked our elusive trio of friends, the answer to that might still lie ahead.

Not that my opinion mattered to either of them. The fact is I might just as well have been furniture for all the notice they took. Having an audience was clearly not a problem. Evidently neither marine officers nor former pinup girls care much for appearances once their desires are aroused.

It began with her hand on the back of his head as she pulled him into the first of a series of kisses and ended with her bra and his regulation tie entwined on the floor. Her hair, though no longer navel length, was sleek and tinged yellow like old ivory, just as it had been when Klara used to braid it to a soundtrack of Doors albums. Eye shadow and glossed lips stood out in what was otherwise a desert of fairness, the effect exaggerated further by the glow of the electric bulb.

It was more the man's expression that held my attention, though. I had seen it before, that blend of puzzlement and desperation that so often consumes men when they stare into the face of a beautiful woman. Indeed they can't help themselves, or so it seems. It's as if they have to crack a code. They must plunge between the loins of that woman until the enigma in front of them turns into an orgasm. Even then, they don't seem sure of their worth.

That was what I perceived, at any rate, as I watched those two bodies heave in unison. At last there came a series of deep groans, and the movement slowed and then subsided, replaced by the sibilation of interlocking mouths.

"Was good for you?" he whispered as he sat up. Diane sighed and then giggled faintly, which apparently was enough to make him feel he'd at least made a start as a code breaker.

"Amazing," he said, stroking her still bare breasts. "Out of this world. Out of this cosmos."

Then he suddenly remembered he had duties elsewhere, and he left the cabin with an assurance that he'd be ready for more the following night.

After he'd gone, I stopped any pretense of being asleep and began to interrogate Diane.

"So was it worth it? I mean, in terms of any information he had."

"Yeah, actually . . ." Diane let her voice fade out. Her lips curled into a smug smile. Smugness was not unexpected. Now that we were re-acquainted, I was noticing that smugness had largely replaced the neophyte's reticence of old. But it wasn't something that Diane usually put on display like this.

"Well, tell me more," I said.

"Seems that Reynard had a shipboard romance." Triumph broke out across Diane's face. The show of emotion was quite a surprise to me.

"Someone else, you mean?" I asked. "Other than Klara and Anton?"

A faint glint in the eyes and a few words of confirmation were all I received in response. Apparently I would have to wait for a full account.

"I need to get some sleep," she concluded with a giggle. "That was hard work."

At breakfast, when the four of us swapped notes, Roderick couldn't resist asking the obvious.

"Male or female? You never know with Reynard."

"He seemed as if he wasn't sure how to explain," replied Diane, referring to her suitor of the night before. "He was a bit strange about it, really. Like he didn't want to talk about it."

Roderick was scathing.

"Wasn't sure? Was this mystery love interest in disguise then? Or was it a case of one of those transgender jobs who don't reveal the goods until you're already flagrante delicto?"

I decided to offer an alternative suggestion.

"Perhaps Diane's friend of last night was too involved with Klara to know or care what Reynard and Anton were doing."

"I doubt it," Diane said. "Emilio wouldn't be Klara's type at all. Too needy."

After what I'd seen of Diane and her officer on the bunk bed a few hours previously, I couldn't help blurting out a retort.

"Looked like he was capable of getting just what he needed."

"I was doing it for the cause, wasn't I?" Diane said with a sharp glance at me.

"Well, we don't have much longer before we leave the ship," Greta said, making it clear by her tone that she expected this to be the final word on the subject, at least until we'd all had a chance to catch up on our sleep and prepare for yet another meal. "Tonight we can have another go at finding out what Emilio knows. There's a toga party in the bar, according to the ship's program. Should be a chance to mingle with the crew again."

CHAPTER FOUR

U p on the promenade deck, I sprawled on a chaise lounge with a towel wrapped around me as a shield against the breeze. In my lap lay a novel, a light-hearted romp involving nymphs and satyrs at a riverside mansion, but I couldn't concentrate.

The prospect of the evening's toga party — apparently a fixture on such cruises — took my mind back to the parties Reynard used to organize.

That's where I first saw Anton. He was such a wall flower.

The place Reynard called home at that time wasn't, in itself, much to get excited about. Suburban red brick semidetached on a quiet street a few minutes' walk from the center of a small town with historic connections and a lively commuter trade with the capital. Two floors and an attic bedroom. A back garden choking on grass and shrubs, with a summerhouse so overshadowed by trees that it had long ago forfeited its original purpose.

Roderick shared the rent, which entitled him to a bedroom of his own. Greta lived there too for a while, although what she contributed and to whom, and what that entitled her to, is a little unclear in retrospect. Part of the time she was Reynard's fiancée, so that accounts for some of it.

In any case, when Reynard and Roderick threw one of their parties, the notion of boundaries largely went out of the window. The house was wall-to-wall people, most of whom I hardly knew and some of whom I wasn't sure I wanted to. They brought with them a fragrance of irregularity, not to mention illegality, and talked in furtive fragments about the price of pills.

Between them, Reynard and Roderick knew everyone, even Klara's entourage. It wasn't surprising really, considering what they did for a living. Reynard was a reporter for the local paper; Roderick was a booking agent for up-and-coming groups in the area. Klara was attending university, on and off, but her expertise was more in the sphere of social contacts. Having parents high in the ranks of who-to-know didn't hurt. At any rate, she rivaled Reynard in her ability to uncover diamonds in the rough and find the glitter in them.

It took someone with that sort of insight to see much glitter in Anton at that point in his life. There was a dichotomy about him that was easy to dismiss as mental weightlessness. He still had that erect boarding school look, with the parted hair and the white shirts and slacks. But peel back that layer, and there was a rebel and romantic waiting to break out. *What's real about him and what isn't,* I remember thinking.

Anyway, it was at a party that Anton's light began to shine. He told me later how he happened to be there. He'd met Reynard at one of those sandwich courses, as they called them. Are they still around? I suppose they must be. Anton was a fresh recruit to the working world, and the newspaper he was apprenticed to sent him to a college for an intensive few weeks in libel law, shorthand, and other skills. Then back to the job—hence the sandwich. Reynard had come by his own reporting career, on a neighboring daily, after four or five years experimenting with life, and was dispatched on the same course.

"I immediately saw something out of the ordinary about Reynard," Anton told me a couple of years after that party, when he was a bit more confident around us. "He stood apart from the other students and sort of studied them, as if he was picking out who he wanted to associate with.

"Well, he picked out me, but at first I didn't feel the same way toward him at all. I thought he had a rather strange stare, a bit intimidating really. My feelings only changed when he began to tell me about Klara.

"I wasn't long out of boarding school, so perhaps you can appreciate my state of mind. You dream of girls like Klara. It's like a reversal of the knight on the white horse stereotype. I was in desperate need of rescue by damsel."

Rescue from what? He didn't say, and I didn't press the point. What is it you want to be rescued from when you're in your late teens? A fear of normal routine perhaps, with its prospect of no knights, no damsels, no white horses. Just nine to five for a very long time. Anyway, I just let him talk.

"So," he went on, "when Reynard showed me photos of this stunning woman and told me how he'd gone on a Mediterranean holiday with her, I could hardly take it in. It was like a fairy story. I was hooked."

Anton was still under that spell when Reynard invited him home from the college where they were sandwiching. That was the weekend of the party, and the rental house hardly had space for the continuous surges of bodies and excitement. How the neighbors tolerated it never entered our heads. Perhaps someone had tipped them off and they'd all left for a peaceful tramp along some distant byway. On the other hand, they might have joined the party. Few would have noticed the difference.

In the build-up to the evening's extravaganza, our little clique lazed around in the summerhouse, which had a sort of ashram ambiance, with velvet cushions instead of chairs and solarized posters shimmering in the candlelight and the atmosphere misted by joss sticks and meandering guitar solos from speakers doubling as supports for a bookshelf.

There was smoking and drinking of various substances, as usual, while the host did his best to impress his special guest with his knowledge of the world. A book containing Salvador Dali prints was a minor revelation to our neophyte, I remember. All those melting clocks and poolside reflections. Quite a sight, especially if it's the first time you've encountered them. Perhaps they don't cover that type of thing in boarding school curricula.

Klara made a fleeting, not to say sweeping, appearance, resplendent as usual in purple boots and fake fur. Reynard observed that her tea bag looked like a spent condom, which was worth a titter from the rest of us but clearly stunned Anton with its audacity.

Later Reynard was brazen enough to lead Anton into his upstairs bedroom. Roderick and Greta and I watched through the open doorway as Anton resisted an attempt at a kiss. We could hear Reynard pressing his case. How transfixed he was by Anton's innocence. How he knew he was asking for a great deal, how it would lift their friendship to new levels, how he'd never be able to repay this gift he was asking Anton to bestow. Unspoken, but pivotal from Anton's perspective I suspect, was the implication that friendship with Klara was part of the package.

Reynard slipped a finger between Anton's reluctant lips. Once they parted, the kiss followed. It was enough, for the time being. There was a glint in Reynard's eyes, and Anton's lean torso succumbed to surrender. Speaking for myself, I never doubted that the ramparts had been permanently breached.

After that, parties became a fairly frequent weekend occurrence, with Anton being an overnight guest whenever his editors' duty rosters allowed. Reporting on two-day cricket matches was a particular bugbear in this respect, and was responsible for several no-shows when rain failed to stop play in time for Anton to catch the evening train.

Whoever invented toga parties must have had only one thing in mind, and that is progressive unraveling and re-attaching. Depending on the intoxicants available, the procedure is liable to be helped along, in the case of attractive young or semi-young women, by a retinue of casual male acquaintances.

Thus, Emilio and his fellow duty officers, securely wrapped in their uniforms, were on hand to smooth and tuck any loose ends as passengers began to drift on to the dance floor after dinner.

"Here, let me help you with this bit over your shoulder," Emilio said to Greta as she fidgeted by the bar. His hand glided over bare skin as he secured the offending corner of sheet. "There, you look like a proper Roman."

He flashed a grin at Diane, as if to say *I'll get to you later,* and then waltzed off to attend to official business.

"Looks like he has designs on both of you tonight," Roderick said, leaning against the counter in a pose more modern suburban than classical.

"Well, I've done my bit," said Diane, whose focus seemed to have switched to a more senior officer.

"How about it then, Greta?" Roderick asked. "Want to have a go at our friend Emilio? With a bit of prodding, so to speak, he might remember something more about this other person who Reynard apparently hooked up with. Or who was dancing with Klara. Maybe there's another clue there."

No sooner had Roderick issued his challenge than Greta was gliding over to the doorway where Emilio and fellow officers were conducting a meet and greet.

"Amazing what people will do with strangers, isn't it," Roderick observed as we watched her go. "I mean, given the right circumstances—a cruise ship for example—and it's like they have a personality transplant. One minute they're all prim and proper, and the next they're hot to trot."

Just as well, I felt. Someone had to do it, if our quest was to make progress. All the same, Roderick's remark seemed to harbor a hint of resentment. Voyeurism was all very well, he might have been thinking, but there was nothing to beat the real thing.

Revelers straggled through a gauntlet of crisp white uniforms. Many clutched togas still in need of expert adjustment. Emilio was quick to oblige, at least as far as the female portion of the throng was concerned. His empathetic smile, dark eyes and tanned cheeks earned him appreciative caresses. No question he was handsome.

Greta was methodical, I'll give her that. All the same, those clear blue eyes and that perfectly contoured face sometimes gave me the creeps. She didn't even use any make-up to speak of, except for a bit around the eyes and lips. It seemed more sculpture than human at times. You had to wonder. Was she as candid and matter-of-fact as she appeared, or was there a cauldron of emotions bubbling in there somewhere?

"This should be interesting," Roderick observed. "Ice woman meets Latin Lothario."

"Not exactly celebrity grudge match material, if you ask me," Diane said. "Not sure what the Lothario bit is all about, but he's not very Latin—I can tell you that."

Roderick scoffed.

"Had a non-Latin technique in the sack, did he?"

"Very funny. Actually, he was pretty good in that department, if you must know. No, his name's not even Emilio. One of the bartenders was telling me. It's like that's his working name. He's really Arnold, or something like that."

"Sort of like tech support people then," Roderick said. "You know, how Mustapha or whoever becomes Bill when he's on the phone with a customer. Only, in Arnold's case, the client gets emotional support. Well, perhaps technical too."

We continued to call him Emilio all the same. Arnold just

wouldn't have had the right cache. Besides, whatever Greta was calling him seemed to be working wonders. Emilio had stepped away from his post to escort her to a secluded booth. A raised arm, with its flash of insignia, brought a waiter hurrying to their alcove.

Watching the couple begin to feel each other out, if that's the right way to put it, I couldn't help pondering on the relative assets of our female bait. Both Diane and Greta had that come-hither-if-you-dare aura about them that men find so challenging, and hetero women — the less charitable ones anyway — find so irritating. It manifested itself in completely different ways, however.

Diane, when she was under Klara's tutelage, was as withdrawn and breakable as one of those sad china angels people put on mantelpieces. With time, she had developed a defiance that made her body seem taut and her expressions brittle. She was still as graceful and trim as a gymnast. But even her friends knew to approach only on her terms.

As for Greta, she had always fascinated me. The few years that had gone by since our little clique's golden age had accentuated her curves. Her proportions were certainly not out of line, though. She still drew more than her share of glances.

The main thing that struck me, though, was that she was so unassuming, so nonchalant about the gifts nature had given her. Whether man or woman, you just wanted to get to grips with her, make those pupils shine with excitement or surprise or . . . anything. I'd give a lot to hear her exclaim passionately. Okay, well I had heard *that* a few times, I'll agree.

Greta sat in that booth like royalty, allowing Emilio to put his hand on her forearm and then, once he saw that that was acceptable, gingerly rake his fingers through her hair. Another officer joined them — one whom I could imagine might call himself Siegfried or Otto, in view of his fair complexion, but who was really Brad or Justin from Chiswick or

Hammersmith. Anything to seem more exotic.

"Looks like Greta has her hands full." Roderick was on the verge of gloating. For a brief minute, the prospect of Greta in a compromising situation was evidently worth more to him than mere information gleaned about the fate of our friends. He turned to Diane. "You might have to step in as backup."

"Not on your life," was the curt response. Diane had bigger quarry — as we would later realize. "In fact, Roderick, I need to hide out in your cabin in case Emilio tries to track me down for a repeat of last night."

Roderick gaped at her for a couple of seconds before replying.

"So, what was wrong with last night?"

"You don't have a clue, do you?" The disgust was still clouding her face as she strutted out of the room. Her final words on the subject drifted back to us in a cold fog.

"Why don't you find a lifeboat to sleep in for tonight, Roderick? I'll need some space."

We were both a little shocked as she moved out of view. Tiffs were not unknown in our circle, but they weren't usually quite so personal. Roderick, struggling to account for Diane's disdain, began to expound on a theory that it had to do with the time of the month. Not a good line of inquiry to pursue, I warned him, and it was dropped without further mention.

In any case, at the far side of the room, Greta seemed to be progressing capably without need of reinforcement. Emilio and his colleague returned briefly to their welcoming duties at the door, and Roderick was able to breeze over to Greta's table and warn her that Diane had commandeered their cabin for the night. Other than that, we just let Greta get on with it.

Meanwhile revelers in their sheets continued to come unraveled to the rhythm of disco classics.

Next to me, Roderick maintained a slightly-off-perpendicular stance against the bar, pretending to be above it all, particularly the music.

"Thank God for cruise ships," he said, raising his voice to compete with the thump of drum machines. "Where else would you hear this stuff outside supermarket aisles and CIA torture chambers?"

But even he succumbed to one of those snake dances—not with snakes gripped between their teeth, I don't mean that, not like the Hopi Indians. I mean one of those dances in which a person grips the hips or waist of the one in front and everyone rumbas or mambos round the room as if they were in a queue in which the queuers had suddenly lost it.

Last I saw of Roderick that night was with his loins polishing the derriere of a rather tipsy woman with an elegant auburn perm. (If perms could speak, this one would undoubtedly have been crying out in embarrassment at its predicament.) She in turn was clinging on to her husband, who was red-faced, frothing with mirth, and clearly oblivious to the coupling behind him.

Eventually I called it a night and left the reverie in the wake of Greta and her two admirers. I could see them heading for the promenade deck, while I made my way back to my cabin. Whether I should expect Roderick to stumble in at some point I wasn't sure. It would depend, I imagined, on how seriously he took Diane's jibe about sleeping in a lifeboat. That, and how well he got on with that couple ahead of him in the dance line.

It must have been about three o'clock when I was awakened by thuds in the corridor. There was a night light glowing dimly on the cabin wall. But not wishing to chance Roderick or anyone else scrambling into my bunk in a drunken haze, I'd opted once again to spend the night on the couch. It was actually roomier than the bunks.

When the door opened, I expected to see Roderick dance an alcoholic hornpipe across the limited floor space and then collapse with a wheeze among pillows and blankets. Instead, I had a perfect view of Greta sandwiched between Emilio and his colleague, Greta's waist and shoulders wrapped in the men's arms. They shuffled toward the lower bunk, looking like contestants in an X-rated three-legged race. Emilio's shirt was unbuttoned, revealing a well-toned chest lightly adorned with hair. The other man was panting. I could only guess whether it was as the result of something he'd done or in anticipation of what he hoped to do.

Of the three, Greta seemed the most in command as they sat on the edge of the bunk. But even she took no notice of me. I might just as well have been watching a TV, with them on the far side of a camera in a studio miles away.

Things progressed the way they usually do, except in this case of course it was in stereo. First Emilio ventured a kiss on the cheek, and then his friend lunged for Greta's neck. With Greta's toga barely covering her, it wasn't long before both pairs of male lips were firmly attached to nipples.

Greta arched her back, pushing forward her throat and her breasts and letting her hair dangle. She'd worn a necklace displaying a jeweled pendant with some sort of ancient-world motif. I'd intended to ask her about it earlier in the evening. Anyway, it flashed sporadically in the light, and Emilio noticed.

"Sexy," he said. "A fertility thing, is it?"

Greta smiled. "It's a talisman," she said. "It takes you under its spell and you have to confess."

"Confess what?"

"Confess your darkest secrets," Greta said, still smiling and with a flutter of eyelashes. It wasn't at all like her to play this kind of game, but perhaps it was her way of trying to get Emilio to open up and tell what he knew about Reynard and Klara. Emilio was either too blank to get it or he just didn't want to cooperate.

"I'm confessing that I want to make love to you," he said. His colleague, apparently a man of few words, continued to snuffle as his tongue descended toward Greta's navel.

Greta let Emilio kiss her with an open mouth. I could see her cheek swell to accommodate his tongue. With one hand in each man's lap, she massaged the ridges now grown prominent beneath their flies. Her fingers, slender and tipped with French polish, were such perfect instruments of control. I have to admit to a vicarious thrill as I watched them slide under waistbands and tangle in pubic curls. The men were eager to facilitate. Zips were undone, underwear pulled down, and Greta curled her right thumb and index finger, with its gold ring glittering, around the base of Emilio's penis.

A rare expression of anticipation followed as Greta's lips hovered above the quivering column. Her tongue flicked across the head, the way you might taste test a frozen treat on a stick. And then her hair trailed across Emilio's thighs like a bridal veil, and the only way I could measure what was happening under it was a loop of deep groans.

Before Emilio had a chance to climax, Greta sat up and pushed him back across the bunk so that he was lying flat with his penis as stiffly exposed as a lone mast on a tranquil sea. In a moment she was astride him, with her back toward his face, and all that could be seen of Emilio's genitalia were balls dancing in time to Greta's bobbing.

She was no less commanding toward her other suitor, who by now had shed his uniform and was standing by her side, no doubt wondering where he fitted in. With her left hand, she guided his penis to her mouth and began probing its tip with her tongue just as thoroughly as she had done with Emilio's. It was shorter, but a little thicker than the one she now had inside he,r and I admired the determination and technique as she stretched her lips around its base.

Evidently her partners had a similar appreciation. Almost

in tandem their pelvises began to buckle in time to a chorus of aahs and oohs. Even in the subdued light, I could see pearly rivulets dribbling down Greta's chin and into the crack between her buttocks, and I mused on whether it had been as good for her as it plainly had been for them. With Greta, it was sometimes difficult to tell.

The three of them slumped across the bunk in a post-coital torpor. But after trying so hard to get as close as possible to Greta in the pre-coital stage, the men began to complain about how stuffy and cramped they were in that confined space.

"I suppose we ought to be getting back to our own quarters," Emilio said. "Could be a bit awkward if we're discovered spending the night in a passenger's cabin."

"Awkward for whom?" I wanted to ask. I was still voyeur incognito though, so I refrained. Besides, I was not aware of either passengers or crew members being forced to walk the plank for sexual indiscretions.

In any case, Greta seemed glad for them to go. She'd done what she intended to do. Emilio and friend bustled down the passageway back to safer territory, and Greta looked slightly startled when I spoke. No doubt she'd forgotten I was there.

"So, any joy?" I asked. Somehow I never phrase it right on these occasions. "I mean, did they tell you anything much?"

A dismissive shake of Greta's head confirmed her interrogations hadn't been satisfactory.

"Emilio said something about the woman with Klara," she said. "I asked him *You mean guy, don't you?*"

With his hair long, Anton did get mistaken for a girl sometimes.

"Emilio just looked blank," Greta continued. "I think Klara he could spot anywhere. But for him, males more or less blend into the crowd—although he did remember Reynard for some reason."

"You think Emilio made a play for Klara?"

"What cruise line officer wouldn't? You can see what he's like. If he did, though, I think he ended up empty handed. He didn't seem to know much more about her, other than how she looked."

Next morning, around brunch time in the ship's well-stuffed schedule of gastric opportunities, Roderick staggered toward me on the promenade deck. Both of us could have done with more sleep. Greta was still down below catching up on her rest.

"So the lifeboat wasn't too comfortable then?" I began.

"Lifeboat? Oh no, I found alternative accommodation."

With a little encouragement, I was sure, he would spill the details. But I truly didn't want to know.

"Seen Diane?" I asked.

"That's an interesting subject," Roderick said with a snigger. If I wasn't going to let him gloat about his own exploits, he'd opt for Diane's. "I went back to the cabin this morning, for a change of clothes. No one was there. Just a toga and a shirt lying on the floor. And you'll never guess what the insignia was on the shirt . . ."

"No, and I probably don't want to," I said. "But let's find Diane, and see what she's prepared to tell us. Don't forget, you were the one who suggested we take this line of inquiry."

"Oh yeah," Roderick assured me. "Not saying for a minute she was doing anything wrong, whoever he was that she was with. You never know who will tell you what, given the right incentive. And let's face it, if anyone knew anything, it was probably him."

We found Diane in the dining room. Brunch was a buffet, but evidently at the captain's table guests merely had to mention their desires in order for morsels to appear on platters in front of them. Lesser mortals like Roderick and I had to jostle in front of a long table of trays and cauldrons, and then munch patiently at a peripheral booth until more favored beings came over to communicate.

"God, you've lucked into the good life," was Roderick's greeting to Diane when she finally came over and sat with us.

"Yeah, well, I had to work for it," Diane responded with a glance at her beau of the night before, now in a fresh uniform at the head of the table. She looked tired, and though her appearance was presentable, there wasn't much artistry to it. Definitely a morning-after look.

"OK," I said. "Did you pick up anything? I mean . . . Well, you know what I mean."

"Actually, I did." Diane couldn't help herself. The daggers of our last encounter with her, at the toga party, turned into an eyeful of ploughshares.

"The captain remembers Klara of course," she said with a grin. "She made quite an impression the day they landed. She'd put together one of those fascinator-type hats. Got the woman in the souvenir shop to help with materials and so forth."

Roderick interrupted with a laugh.

"Just like Klara. Quite a sight coming down the gangplank, I'll bet," he said. "Must have caught a few eyes, besides the captain's."

Diane nodded before continuing.

"When they make port, or whatever the phrase is, it's a big deal apparently. Not everyone does the return trip. Passengers like us leave the ship, and even some of the crew. Anyway, that's what Reynard and Klara and Anton did . . . And the thing is, there was a woman with them."

"Someone Reynard picked up probably," Roderick said. I was about to add that it could equally as well have been someone Klara picked up, but it seemed disrespectful in front of Diane.

"Apparently it caused quite a stir among the crew," Diane

continued. "What with Klara looking the way she does and this dark beauty—that's what the captain called her—on Reynard's arm."

"Well a brunette would make a change for him, after Klara and Greta." Roderick talked as if he could read Reynard like a book. "But whoever said he didn't like variety."

"I think it was more than hair though," Diane said. "From what the captain said, it was more her complexion."

As usual, Roderick had the answer.

"Oh, like maybe she came from this part of the world, and so they hooked up with her on board."

"Well that's what I thought at first," Diane confirmed. "But then the captain said something about the four of them meeting up at one of their ports of call. I asked him to check the passenger list, 'cos I thought he must be making a mistake. But sure enough, this woman had joined them part way through the voyage, like it had all been thought out ahead of time. So, what do you make of that?"

CHAPTER FIVE

Our plans for what to do after we reached the mainland were vague, to say the least. First of all, of course, we had to get to the island. Then, if there *were* bodies — and I still had my doubts about that — they would be in a morgue somewhere, presumably. That's what happens in the movies, anyway.

But when you don't speak the language and don't have an official badge to flash, you feel so much more helpless than some glamorous actor or actress with a script and a director making sure the rest of the cast do what they're told.

I suppose that's why we experienced what you might call "mission drift."

"Let's head into the city," Roderick counseled as our vessel dispatched us on the quay. "We'll likely find the best bargains for hotels and food there."

Even though there'd been plenty of people around us on the ship, a busy port with cars and noise everywhere took some getting used to. It was a while before we got our land legs, so to speak, and stopped swaying as if the concrete under us was about to break into a swell.

Slowly we adjusted to the activity on the dock. With our few days of relatively relaxed routine at an end, there was no recourse. Disembarking passengers and crew flowed past our quartet with bewildering speed and purpose. We peered around for officials or signs or anything to give us direction. Was this how it had been for Reynard and Klara? It was hard to conceive of either of them being flustered. Perhaps the dark lady had already made arrangements for their arrival.

We collected our luggage and gaped like abandoned fledglings in the direction of transport options. We were still a distance from the capital, and the warehouses and passageways around us had the ambiance of places where strangers come to grief. A couple of taxis offered the quickest exit.

With relief, we alighted a half hour later in surroundings more suited to visitors yearning for mod cons and a breathing space. After consulting the city's tourist authorities, we found modest but satisfactory lodging in a district of clean, narrow streets. It was an older area, and its earth-toned facades and wrought-iron verandahs were largely outside the realm of commuter traffic.

We were, the hotel concierge assured us, within "easy walking distance" of the antiquities for which the city was famous. What's more, there were several alleys leading to bars with open-air courtyards where waitresses would bring us munchies and local brew and small ensembles entertained with obscure stringed instruments and operatic male voices.

It was hard to avoid a twinge of guilt on our first evening as we reclined around a table at first one and then another of these back-alley establishments. As Greta put it, "We mustn't lose sight of why we're here."

"Not at all," Roderick said between gulps of liquid refreshment. "But we need to acclimatize. It could be important in helping us understand the cultural context for what happened to Klara and the others. I mean, now we suspect they had a native of these parts with them, it could change the whole picture."

Diane looked glum. Evidently she took Roderick's reasoning at face value. I was inclined to see it more as an excuse for continuing revelry.

"Let's not jump to conclusions," she said. "The captain could've got it wrong about them knowing her. The dark beauty could have been someone they came across while she was checking in, or whatever you call it with boats. And she might have waved goodbye to them as soon as they headed inland."

"Listen," Roderick countered, "if Reynard has a woman on his arm, he's not going to let her go till he's good and ready."

There was a lapse in conversation after that. If anyone would know about Reynard's romantic inclinations, it was Greta. But she just sat erect, sipping suds and staring at the musicians with that impenetrable serenity she had when she wasn't inclined to reveal much. Perhaps Roderick had a point though, in his gauche way. If Reynard had had a relationship with this dark beauty onboard and then they'd left arm in arm, it would be unlike him to meekly bid farewell.

The next day we surrendered to the distractions of stone columns and finely chiseled human appendages. Our pilgrimage to hallowed sites, each one partnered by an interpretive museum, reminded me of childhood Sundays, when the need for rites was as much of a mystery as the rites themselves. It was just something that had to be done. Still, despite the exertion, we paid our respects and by the end of the day were glad we did.

For all our technology, I don't think we have come any closer to an appreciation of the human physique than those sculptors of the ancient world. Statues and fragments of statues stood on display in all sizes. Some of them looked a little weathered, it's true, and a few had limbs missing. But you could tell how dynamic they must once have been.

Alongside lofty freestanding relics, glass cases held a menagerie of manikins and, if there is such a term, girlikins. Many were in the most agile and graceful poses, so that you couldn't help feeling that this was a civilization which really understood bodies and what they were capable of.

We paused before larger-than-life marble figures on

platforms and pedestals, then paced around to see if their rear ends were as appealing as their front exposures. They were. Those smoothly-polished posteriors, we agreed, were the work of people who must have known a thing or two about buttocks.

"I hate to point it out though," Roderick said, keeping his volume down so as not to disturb other museum patrons. "The guys seem to be a little on the small side at the front, don't you think? I mean, even the gods. You'd expect them to be pretty well equipped, with all the siring of mortal offspring going on back then."

"Only *you* would think it's all down to size," Diane responded. "They probably had techniques you can only dream about."

"Well, what about the women then?" Roderick persisted. "I mean, I'm not a big breast man myself, but I like a little to hold on to. It's pretty obvious these girls had never encountered silicone."

Diane and Greta exchanged nearly identical expressions, consisting of arched brows, rolling eyes, and pouting lips.

"Just joking, ladies," Roderick tried to assure them. "It's what's inside that matters. I know that."

"I think you better shut up before some flat-chested bint overhears you and you get clobbered," Diane said, resisting any urge to join in with Roderick's sniggers.

Unaccustomed though we were to the heat, we walked along the main tourist routes well into the late morning. In dark glasses and hat and long sleeves and sunscreen, I almost felt like one of those people in protective suits who you see on TV in disaster areas. Sunlight dazzled us from every manmade surface, and we played a sort of hopscotch game hurrying from one shady tree to the next. Not that the trees gave much shade. A lot of them were the thin pointy type, like poplars.

Eventually we came to a huge amphitheater, which took away what little breath we were still able to gasp. Our weariness seeped away as we marveled at a dozen aspects of what we were viewing.

"Just look at the precision," Roderick began. "And the artistry, and the workmanship."

"And even the way," Diane said, "it looks as if an ancient orator in a toga could walk right into the middle of it and start spouting classical stuff — like he'd just popped out for a sandwich at halftime."

"It makes them seem very close, those people who lived back then," said Greta, and indeed it did. The surface things have changed of course, but the needs and urges can't have been so different. And despite Roderick's museum critique, the human body probably looks and feels much the same. At least, I'd like to imagine so.

The part of the amphitheater where the audience sat was so steep we had to watch our footing as we descended to the stage area. That's why we didn't see earlier that there was a familiar face sharing our experience. Roderick caught sight of him first.

"That looks a bit like that officer fellow on the ship," he said, peering across the rows of stone seats at a figure in the shadow of an archway. We got nearer, and the figure sauntered further under the arch. There was enough of a profile, though, for Greta and Diane to both nod in confirmation. Something about sleeping with someone — or at any rate lying prone with them — makes them easier to spot, even in a crowd.

"That's Emilio, I feel pretty sure," Diane agreed, "although he doesn't seem so familiar now he's out of uniform."

"That's not what I heard," Roderick said with a leer.

"Strange he didn't see us," I said. "We're pretty exposed up here in the dress circle."

We were still looking down as we crossed the intricately patterned stage. Fear of tripping over a two-thousand year old pothole kept us, almost literally, on our toes. When we finally reached the archway, Emilio—if indeed it had been him—was gone.

For a lingering moment or two, it brought Anton to my mind. When we first knew him particularly, he'd often lurk on the periphery of whatever was going on, hardly more than a shadow.

He was so slim back then, I remember, and his head would droop a little, so that his hair curtained off his face. Whatever his expression was, you couldn't really tell. Roderick thought that it was mixed company that made Anton bashful.

"All those years in male dormitories probably played tricks with his mind, not to say his body," Roderick observed to me one day when Anton wasn't around to hear.

Roderick might have been on the right track. He was sometimes.

Of course, if it suited him, Reynard could quickly usher his reluctant disciple into the inner circle, bringing Anton into the fold as if he were a trim and elegant sacrificial lamb.

Reynard would turn on that earnest, seductive beam of admiration he'd perfected, and Anton couldn't resist. It was like being summoned to a podium to receive some award, like an Oscar or a Tony. All Anton could do, as he accepted the accolades, was murmur his undying gratitude. Late at night, the murmurs from both of them would become rather more animated. But those of us who heard reckoned it was all consensual.

In any case, it was pretty clear to all of us except perhaps Reynard that what Anton was really waiting for was a knowing wink from Klara. In that, he wasn't alone. Even after Diane arrived on the scene, there were plenty, male and female, who got a thrill, brief but intense, from some morsel of attention Klara gave them. Making her laugh or feeling her slightest touch was positively orgasmic, judging by their expressions.

In that respect, Anton was more fortunate than the majority. Klara took an interest in him from the start. Whether that was born of covetousness because Reynard had adopted him, I don't know. The deity of erotic possibilities, whichever one that is, was ever lurking in that household. That was just before Klara uncovered Diane, so it's hard to fathom motives.

One thing for sure, both Reynard and Klara got their kicks from seduction. For Klara, as opposed to Reynard, it didn't necessarily have to result in out-and-out coitus. She just wanted to know that total surrender was hers for the taking. Perhaps it's like those mountain climbers who say they do it *because it's there.*

Exactly how the relationship between Reynard and Anton developed in its early stages I'm not sure. But, from the latter's viewpoint, it had its frustrations. I do know that.

"The second time I visited Reynard," Anton told me once, "there was another big party at his house. I was late. Another of those unending cricket matches I had to report on.

"Anyway, first person I saw when I walked in was Klara coming down the stairs. Her face lit up at the sight of me, I swear, and of course that sent chills up and down my spine — and a couple of other places too.

"She took my hand and led me up to the landing, and I was thinking *Oh God, I'm on the stairway to nirvana.* All that purple she wore was making me weak at the knees, along with memories of the texture of her lipstick and the gleam of her nails. Soon to be brushing up against my naked skin, I thought.

"Yeah, in my wildest dreams, it turned out. Instead of leading me into a private cubby hole as I'd fantasized, she pushed open the door to an attic room, and there were her friends sitting round in a circle smoking pot. I suppose she just saw me as another addition to the gathering.

"I think I left after a minute or so and went to look for Reynard. But it was one of those moments when a situation is in the balance. I should have just bustled her into a cupboard or somewhere and at least told her how I felt. You only think later of what you should have done though, don't you."

Even back then, when I heard this, I didn't feel too sorry for Anton. I'm guessing that, in subsequent encounters, Klara more than made up for keeping him waiting. Pure speculation of course. Well, make that impure.

CHAPTER SIX

Despite good intentions, we lingered too long in the city. A lifestyle of late breakfasts and languid lunches ensnared us and, to be fair, our leads in the case of the missing trio did not point to an instant course of action. It was all too easy to lapse into contemplation and calls for more research.

As usual, Diane, Roderick and I were sitting around a table in one of those back alley bars, unwinding at the end of the day. Greta had gone to find out about ferries to the islands, and we were waiting for her to join us for dinner.

Time was pressing on, we kept remarking to each other in so many words. All the same, it was hard to resist the counterproductive force of bouzoukis and beer.

"Maybe we shouldn't leave here in too much of a hurry until we've heard something more from the police," Roderick said.

Diane, whose devotion to Klara was still hard to gauge, thought otherwise.

"The police?" she said, her lips puckering into a snarl. "If we wait for them to tell us anything, we'll be here long enough to look for Klara's grandchildren."

"Now that's an interesting image," was Roderick's reply in the wake of a deep gulp of lager. "It would be like a new breed of Sirens. Sailors in these parts would see a purple haze on the horizon, and the next thing they'd know, their boats would be smashed on rocks and they'd be sharing a pipe with a tribe of red-haired maidens."

The topic was silly enough to offer some diversion from

death and disappearance, and I was about to add to it by asking where Klara's male grandchildren might fit into this vision. Fortunately Greta's arrival cut me off.

Her eyes cast downward, she hurried across the space in front of the musicians — dance floor, I suppose you'd call it, although it didn't seem to have a set purpose. I turned to watch. Anxiety was not what I expected from Greta.

"What's up?" I asked, expecting details about boats or buses.

"He's here," she said as she sat down. We stared at her blankly. "Emilio. He's over by the bar. Or at least was when I came in."

"Do you think he knows we're here?" Roderick asked. "Seems like quite a coincidence that we'd see him, or think we saw him, at the amphitheater — and now here he is again."

"Perhaps we should re-introduce ourselves," I said. "I mean, I could see him not remembering Roderick and me. But . . ."

"Yeah, he was pretty besotted with you two, wasn't he," Roderick piped in, looking first at Diane and then Greta. "Hard to believe he's in a bar with two of the loves of his life and he doesn't even offer to buy you a drink."

Diane was squinting at the familiar backside on a stool by the bar. Well, we all were.

"Looks like he knows he's been seen," she said. "He's in a rush to pay up and go."

"Not if I can help it he won't," said Roderick, who was on his feet and striding toward the bar before the rest of us were able to say another word.

From a distance it was like watching one of those silent films. First Roderick blocked Emilio's exit from the bar. Then Emilio raised his hands as if he wanted to brush his assailant aside. If it had been a movie, there would have been a round of fisticuffs. But gradually the accusative ripples in Roderick's face subsided, to be replaced by a finger pointing toward us and, so we guessed, an insistent invitation to join us at the table.

Emilio turned with a shrug, and actually smiled lamely in our direction as the two men approached.

"Well, pull up a chair," I said. "This is a surprise."

It was hard to know what to say.

"You must think I'm some sort of voyeur," Emilio began, doing a convincing job of combining candor and embarrassment. "You're probably wondering what I'm doing here."

"Yes and yes," said Greta, adding when Emilio didn't catch on immediately, "Yes we did think that, and yes, what are you doing here?"

In blue jeans and a loose patterned shirt, Emilio was as handsome as he had been in uniform. Developed but not overdeveloped muscles seemed to contour his clothes no matter what he wore. But the authority in his manner and expressions had subsided into something more vulnerable and earnest. Actually, it was rather endearing.

"I suppose I should begin by saying that Emilio is not my real name."

"Arnold, isn't it?" Diane chipped in. The person in question nodded.

"Never mind," I said. "I think we've decided we prefer Emilio. It's more romantic. So why don't you stick to it, at least as far as we're concerned."

He smiled in relief as if *Emilio* was his preference all along.

"I'll begin with some background," he started, after we ordered him a beer. "I've been working for the cruise line for a couple of years now. It beats a lot of jobs, what with the perks."

Diane's look of indignation caught his eye.

"What I mean," he hastily continued, "is the tips can be quite sizeable. And you can't beat the weather, can you? Once you get past the English Channel anyway."

"We're not stupid," Diane said. "Obviously the social life on board is an attraction too."

"Well, let's just say it's hard to be lonely," Emilio continued. "It's true, women do like a man in uniform."

"Or out, as the case may be," Roderick muttered.

"The social side of it changed for me though," Emilio went on. "Earlier this year I met a woman from here on a return voyage to England. The first time I saw her—the staircase on the main deck it was, where the bursar's office is—she just stood out as someone very special. Part of it, I think, was her coloring. Dark skin, chestnut eyes, raven hair, and teeth so dazzlingly perfect I was saying hello to her several times a day just so I could see her smile . . . Well, you've been there. You know how it is with the parties aboard, what with the officers mingling with the passengers."

"Yeah, we noticed that you're pretty good at mingling," Roderick interrupted. Emilio shrugged off the remark with a forced chuckle before going on. There still seemed to be a residue of tension between the two men, though.

"Anyway, a relationship developed between us, in the course of which I learned that she comes from a wealthy, prestigious family. Her parents have a castle on one of the islands, and they pretty much run the show there. Helen—that's her name—has a fear of flying."

"Know how she feels," Diane interrupted. Not being privy to Diane's travel preferences, Emilio gave her a glance of minor incomprehension before continuing.

"So that's how she came to be on the ship. Heading for London and Paris, she was, for some R and R."

I was tempted to utter a witticism about our own "two R's"—Reynard and Roderick. But unlike some people I could mention, I don't always blurt out the first thing that comes to mind. Not always, that is. And in this case, just as well I didn't.

"Once we reached London," Emilio continued, "we kept in touch. I had some leave, and I was more than willing to show her the sights. Everywhere we went, she would turn heads. She seemed to expect it. Well, I suppose you would if you looked that good."

He glanced at Diane and Greta, conscious perhaps of the part a thoughtfully delivered compliment might play in enhancing post-coital relations.

"You ladies would know about that, of course . . ."

"Plus she had that wealthy aristocratic thing, by the sound of it," Roderick added. "You can't help noticing that in a woman. Not that I'm saying Diane and Greta don't have their own, more natural qualities."

What might have seemed gauche in Emilio a moment before suddenly seemed gallant by contrast. We turned back to him, genuinely eager to hear more of his story.

"Anyway, to give you the headlines, we were soon an item, so to speak. I couldn't believe my luck, really. A fairly run-of-the-mill fella like me hooking up with a beautiful . . . heiress, you might call her. She talked a lot about her family and their life on the island.

"Before long I had to report back to my ship. While I was away she was going to go to Paris. She'd already made arrangements for her stay before she left home. So there was an emotional farewell, and I left with expectations that we'd pick up where we left off when I got back.

"The itinerary for that voyage was much the same as the one you were on. So I had a bit of time to spare when I got to where we are now. One of the other officers was from here, actually, so while we were ashore, I asked him if he'd heard of Helen's family or knew anything about the island where they lived. I didn't let on that I knew Helen.

"Well, his face dropped and he began to tell me these

stories he'd heard about strange goings-on. Parties and such. Rumors mostly. He had a religious streak, so he didn't want to go into detail."

"Sounds like Reynard and Klara would be right at home," Roderick said with a laugh.

"Yeah, could be. Wait till you hear the rest of it," Emilio said, his tone a grim contrast with Roderick's. "I brooded a bit about what my friend had told me, I'll admit, but I'd more or less dismissed it by the time that tour of duty ended. I was dying to see Helen again.

"I should have known something was up when she wasn't there to meet me, like we'd arranged. I went back to my flat. No sign of her there. I left messages. Nothing doing. Then I went to the hotel where she'd been staying—and who do you think I saw?"

Maybe Greta saw it coming. She could be sharp in her undemonstrative way, and let's face it, personal history gave her particular insight. The rest of us just stared like couch potatoes in front of the telly until Emilio relieved our suspense.

"Your friend Reynard," he said. "Somehow or other they'd met while I was away, and he'd just moved in on her. I watched them together. She was besotted. The next I knew, just to add insult to injury, they'd booked passage on my ship. I don't think she even noticed me anymore, she was so fixated on your friend."

For a moment Emilio turned his attention directly to Diane and Greta.

"Sorry I wasn't more forthcoming on the ship," he said in the soft tones of a genuine apology. "Your questioning about your friends confused me. I didn't quite know what I was getting into."

We had witnessed enough of Emilio's escapades on the ship to suspect he didn't necessarily need to know what he was getting into. Full steam ahead seemed to be more to his liking. But fortunately Roderick refrained from pointing this out, and we maintained silence until Emilio resumed his account.

"The four of them were quite the center of attention, I can tell you, especially that woman with the red hair and the purple lipstick. I just wanted to melt into the bulwarks. I did my job, and — to be honest with you — cried myself to sleep for a night or two. I couldn't believe Helen would ignore me, as if I were a stranger. I suppose that's what love, or whatever you want to call it, can do to people sometimes."

Even Roderick could come up with no witty comment in answer to that.

"Sometimes you just have to let people go," I said at last. Roderick nodded in agreement and indicated his intention to buy another round.

"That's what I thought," Emilio conceded. "Off they went down the gangway. I'm sure the captain told you, Diane, what a pantomime that was. Get over it and move on, I told myself.

"When I got back to London, though, there were messages waiting for me from the answering service. It was Helen. She didn't say much. Just wanted me to call. Her tone was insistent. So I tried. Again and again. But there was never any answer. Then the number was out of order."

"Perhaps you could have tried reaching her parents," Diane said as she sipped one of the fresh brews Roderick had brought.

"Even if I made contact, they don't know me. And there might have been a language barrier. Who knows whether they speak English? No, I thought the best thing to do was take some leave when I reached here on my next voyage and see if I could find out more.

"And that, you see, is when I made contact with you. Once I realized who you were looking for, I could see that you might very well lead me to Helen."

"With a couple of one-night stands on the way," said Roderick, who clearly wasn't trying hard to bond with our fellow searcher.

"It doesn't look very good, I know," Emilio agreed. "But I'm not sure how I feel about her now, or how she feels about me. I'm a bit mixed up. All I know is her messages made it sound as if she was in trouble of some kind. I felt I had to follow up in some way."

Turning on the sincerity, he added: "And I was genuinely attracted to you both, believe me. There was nothing fake about that."

"Yeah, it is definitely harder for men to fake it," confirmed Roderick, never failing to exercise his wit no matter how jaded the topic.

CHAPTER SEVEN

What could we do but invite Emilio to tag along with us? The fate of his ex-fiancée and our friends seemed to be linked, and in any case I think we felt tainted with guilt by association. Reynard had perhaps caused Helen to forsake our new associate, although of course we just had Emilio's version of it. For all we knew, she could have gone to Paris with the notion of being rid of him.

What was undeniable, though, was that Emilio had a better idea of where to look and what we'd find there than we did. Between what his officer friend had told him and his own inquiries, he gave us a pretty clear picture of the island and the illustrious family that lived in a former colonial fortress. He even knew how to get to it, although Greta too had researched the ferries and had even found accommodation for us.

"Well, it's time to move on," Roderick confirmed as we collected our thoughts and luggage outside the hotel. It was a wrench to abandon such a comfortable retreat, but Emilio's disclosures meant that we could no longer put off the next stage in our search.

We waited at a taxi stand for Emilio to meet us while equivocating about what lay ahead.

"Whether all four went together to this island is one consideration," Roderick mused. Even he was losing confidence in an easy solution to the puzzle. "I mean, perhaps Helen did split with them. And then there's still the abandoned boat and the bodies to account for . . ."

"If there ever were bodies," I said.

"Police don't make stuff up," Roderick replied, adding a pointed, "Do they?"

"The one thing we do know is we haven't heard from them since they left," Diane said. "I mean, Klara and me, we're not like we were once, but we still keep in touch. To go on holiday and not phone or send a postcard or anything, it's not like her. It was only going to be for, what, two or three weeks. It's getting on for two months since they left."

"Funny Reynard didn't mention this woman, Helen, when we had that get-together at your flat," Roderick said, gesturing at me. "When he announced this big holiday plan."

"That was months ago," I said. "He may have met her after that. Besides, Reynard sometimes keeps his cards close to his chest. Maybe he hadn't clued in Klara and Anton at that point."

The more I thought about it, the more plausible my argument was. Reynard might easily have held off spilling the beans till it suited him. Yes, he believed in being candid — sometimes with shock being his chief purpose — but telling the truth is not the same as telling the *whole* truth. And there's also the question of when you tell it.

Even as his friend, I recoiled sometimes at the shameless way he manipulated people, even those close to him. *Especially* those close to him. Anton was the prime example. How impressionable he was at first, and how instinctively Reynard took advantage of it.

"I am not worthy of your friendship," Reynard would tell him. What a beguiling line that was for a young mind. Such a responsibility. Perhaps I was a little jealous.

Reynard would bolster his declared admiration for Anton with praise for practically everything he did or said. Anton's poems — anguished mega-metaphors typical of the teen-twenty transition years — were hailed as works of genius. His openness to Reynard's tastes in rock music and 20th century art was "insightful." His physique, as supple and spare as a sapling, prompted a cantata of lust and idolatry.

Egged on like this, Anton veered into a dress sense eccentric even for the time. My perennial image of him remains one of a figure clad in a scarlet-lined cape or green knee-high boots or a broad-brimmed black hat with an ostrich feather protruding from the band, or any one of the other extraordinary items of clothing he acquired with Reynard's encouragement.

Why, such indulgence even extended to bodily functions. For a time, when the house Reynard and Roderick rented was particularly crowded, Reynard and Anton and Klara and Diane shared a bedroom. Each couple had a bed, although exactly where the boundaries were is not part of recorded history. Don't forget, we're talking about a more open-minded time, when young people were apt to accept such arrangements without hesitation. More than likely, it was just a case of who saw what rather than actual bed hopping. After all, Anton's agony in those early days was that Reynard kept the girls just out of his reach — or rather, bearing in mind Anton's bashfulness, him just out of their reach.

Anyway, Reynard had convinced Anton that only physical intimacy between the two of them could preserve his mental faculties, that without the touch of skin upon skin, like a divine anointment, he — Reynard, that is — would find it hard to endure the barrenness, the profound disappointments of this world.

Considering that the pillow talk reported to me emanated from the other set of pillows in the room, I cannot say with certainty how effective this approach was. Reynard, I'm led to understand, did make some concessions in terms of the degree of intimacy required. For instance, there was more of an emphasis on surface contact than on penetration. But the contact, in whatever degree, apparently produced the desired result.

Reynard, the same source revealed, took delight in bringing Anton to a climax with his hand. What particularly impressed him was the great liquid arc that soared forth at that instant, sometimes spouting the length of Anton's torso before plunging to earth somewhere north of his overgrown Beatle cut. I'm no expert, but I'm sure there are quantities of young males who can perform similar feats. Nonetheless, Anton was made to feel that in this he had the makings of a champion. With such a diet of praise, Reynard did indeed make it very painful for his protégés to fall when they inevitably fell from grace.

We arrived once more at the port and, as our taxis deposited us on the edge of the Mediterranean, we rejoiced in the view before us. The gallons of suds we'd downed in the tourist quarter had led to celebration of one sort. But here in front of us was a volume of liquid even more exhilarating.

"What kept us?" Diane asked on behalf of us all, or the majority anyway. "This is what brought us here—not getting plastered in back alley dives."

"Everything has its time," Roderick countered. "First planning, then action."

"Except, before Emilio got involved, I think you were planning on a few more nights carousing before getting to any action," was the retort.

The sea stretched to the horizon like a sheet of turquoise bubble wrap, placid and saturated with color. It was so inviting compared to the chilled and froth-tipped tongues of gray I remembered from childhood seaside holidays.

Tickets had already been purchased, and all that was left to do was to haul our multiple bags on to the ferry.

Naturally, we gravitated to the bar as soon as we were aboard. We sipped pilsners and listened to Roderick yearn for "a pint of real draught ale."

Eventually he moved on.

"Well, Emilio, you seem to have the inside track here. What do we do when we get there?"

Emilio absorbed the residue of sarcasm with a faint smile, and addressed his reply more to the ladies than to his questioner.

"First step I think is to unload and spend the evening decompressing at the hotel Greta booked for us," he said.

"It's a bit away from the main port," Greta said. "So we should have some quiet there, and we can get ourselves together over dinner perhaps."

"Then tomorrow," Emilio continued, "we'll look into renting a car. We might even need two. But one at least—so we can scout around, find out what's going on at the family fortress, whether Helen has been seen around there, that sort of thing. That officer friend I told you about, he gave me some names to look up—people who might be helpful."

"Don't forget the boat, where they found the bodies," Diane intervened.

"Or so rumor has it," I said. I couldn't resist adding that.

"It's over on the other side of the island," Roderick said. "There's a fishing village, and apparently the boat was drifting in a cove nearby."

"You think we'll be able to find out any more from the police?" I asked.

"Could go either way," was Emilio's guess. "At least, based on my experiences on the mainland. Let's face it, the authorities are bound to wonder why we're wandering around asking questions. They don't like anything that seems like interference. From what Helen told me, before . . . well, before we split up that is, the locals can be a bit clannish out here in the islands. Besides, they may not even speak English."

"Well, we'll just have to take it slowly and carefully," Greta advised, prompting Roderick to quip, "Yeah, you ladies can turn on the charm. That seems to have an effect."

For an hour or so our vessel skirted rugged outcrops and headlands devoid of shrub or tree, until we longed for the sight of habitation.

"If not a desert island," Roderick said, "it looks like a deserted one."

"Life here is still a hard scrabble," Emilio informed us. "Inland you'll see much of the farming is done with terraces. As for the coast, you've got to know the lay of the land, so to speak. These rocks have caused more than their share of wrecks, including a few would-be invaders."

"I wonder if that's what got Reynard and Klara, and Anton, into trouble," Diane said.

Roderick took up the theme.

"It's a puzzle really, isn't it," he said. "I mean, none of them had any sailing experience to speak of. I think Reynard and I might have had a go in a dinghy on a reservoir back in our youth. Suddenly here they are taking off on a bloody great sloop, or it whatever it was. They must have had someone with them, don't you think?"

"Like they rented a boat with crew members?" Greta asked.

"Yeah," Roderick agreed, and then, perhaps as a sort of peace offering, he turned to Emilio for a more informed opinion. "You can do that, can't you? Hire a boat with a captain to take care of the steering and navigation?"

"Sure," Emilio said. "It would be the wise thing to do, even for someone with sailing experience. Nothing like having a local aboard."

"Funny that no one ever came forward though," Greta said. "You'd think there'd be reports of missing crew members or something."

"Perhaps they did come forward and we just didn't get to hear about it," I spoke up.

"Or perhaps there are more bodies than we know about," Roderick added.

A vision of the boat becalmed, with its two bodies bobbing alongside like discarded plastic bottles, had haunted me ever since that initial phone call from the reporter. Even based on the barest of information, one of our three friends was unaccounted for. The conversation called further into question what had seemed improbable all along—that they'd sailed off by themselves on a chartered cruise without anyone else having a clue what they were up to. At the very least, there must be a charter company that could account for the boat and, surely, verify whether they were in fact accompanied by a hired captain or crew.

My first sight of our destination made me think of the wasps' nests that hung from the eaves of sheds and barns back home. In the same way as the wasps grafted a row of individual cells, each with its gaping entrance, on to the wood, so these island folk had clung to the curve of the bay as their foundation.

A tight crescent of hotels and shops and other businesses squeezed between water and a backdrop of low slopes rising in undulating layers toward the horizon. From a distance, blocks of condos and lines of houses could have been a child's creation of mounds of mud plastered on the rocks, their windows and doors being holes poked by a stick.

It was a scene both elemental and organic, with the sun dazzling us from waves and whitewash and the entire port stark as an escarpment exposed by wind and time.

Nearing the jetty, we abandoned our beer and mingled on the open deck. As might be expected, passengers segregated into groups of tourists and residents—or, by their more formal clothes and reserved manners, so I assumed the latter to be.

Everywhere there was a sense of anticipation, though, and behavior varied accordingly. Children, with their primary-colored back packs and shrill exclamations, danced around pairs of adults. School groups kept up an internal dialogue at high decibels. Two or three older couples edged into quieter spaces, staring as if paying homage to familiar landmarks, and exchanging comments in a tongue that was altogether foreign to me. I thought back to what Emilio had said about language perhaps being a barrier in our investigations, and realized the barrier could even be impregnable.

"Would it be disrespectful if we looked around the shops?" Diane asked as we stood assembling our thoughts on the quay. "I don't mean now. Tomorrow maybe. I know we have a mission and we're not here to be tourists, but . . ."

"Might be a good idea actually," Roderick said. "It would give us a chance perhaps to ask a few questions. You know, get the lay of the land. And we've got to find out about a rental car anyway."

By then we were becoming aware of something common, probably, to all ports, especially Mediterranean ones—a blonde stranger with luggage is not left alone for long. Two blondes, as we possessed, attracted a paparazzi of taxi drivers, would-be guides to the town's attractions, and distributors of fliers offering shopping and clubbing discounts especially suited, so we were told in clipped English, to beautiful ladies.

"You'd think I didn't exist," said Roderick, who was unaccustomed to such a thought. "For all they know, Emilio and I are your husbands. They're lucky they don't get their snouts re-shaped."

"Do I detect jealousy?" I asked. I was teasing, but also curious. Roderick still seemed a little bent out of shape by

Emilio's presence—and a little unsure, too, of the nature of Emilio's relationship with Greta and Diane. Did shipboard intimacy have consequences when it came to hotel sleeping arrangements? Judging by the unspoken tension in answer to my question, there was general unease on the subject. Testosterone never rests, does it? And maybe that goes for estrogen too.

At life's midway point, if that's what you call approaching forty, we seemed hardly more resistant to the green-eyed devil—jealousy, I mean—than we were at twenty. More cynical about it, yes. Less tender and exposed in our suffering. But victims nonetheless.

Those pangs and uncertainties and insecurities of unrequited love had certainly found a master manipulator in Reynard. How he would play Anton with a casual comment or two.

"Klara likes you," I overheard him say to Anton once. "Lovers can be so easily swayed. She's done it before, taken people away from me. But you mean so much to me. I don't think I could stand it."

What could Anton say? As I recall, he stood there like a puppy willing to roll over to atone for the very thought of transgression. He replied, "I wouldn't do that to you." Reynard gave him a piercing look, and such was the tension in the moment that, had I been religious, I might well have anticipated the third crowing of a cock.

On other occasions, Reynard would take an opposing tack and inform Anton in the most provocative detail of Klara's sexual preferences. For instance, Anton was unable to be present at one of Reynard's birthday celebrations—due no doubt to one of those weekend cricket marathons he had to chronicle.

Reynard was careful, of course, to let him know what he had missed. It just so happened that Klara and Diane were indulging in food sex, that being quite a fad for them at the time. Once the tabloids got hold of rumors about certain celebrities playing affectionately with chocolate bars, eating was never the same. Positions missionary and otherwise had to be garnished and stuffed. Be it confectionary or vegetable, solid or semi-liquid, there seemed to be place for it in, or on, the human body. And once there, the rules of the game suggested it should be sampled or smeared or, in the case of more solid ingredients, applied with friction.

"Klara likes honey on her clit," Reynard told Anton when he next visited. I was in the summerhouse with them. Diane and Klara, needless to say, were not present.

"She says it tickles as it runs down her crack," he continued in a jocular tone one might use for critiquing a soap opera on last night's TV. "Diane's job is to lick it off before it gets on the sheets."

What Reynard didn't say, only implied, was that as the weekend's guest of honor—it being his birthday—he accounted for a few drips of his own. Anton could only smile, as if sharing a sweetener with Klara and Diane couldn't have been further from his desires. Torture or turn-on? It's a bit like S and M, isn't it. Sometimes it's hard to know where to find the dividing line between pleasure and pain. Having one's love interest frolicking around with someone else really gets some people going. Anyway, as I've said before, perhaps Anton's made up for it since.

Accommodation at the hotel, it turned out, was ours for the taking. As were the taxis. Thankfully, the journey there was short and relatively uncomplicated by who sat with whom. I sat next to Greta, but if either of us derived any stimulation by being virtually joined at the hip, it escaped me. As far as I could tell, that applied to the others, too. Even Roderick seemed relatively relaxed.

We drove along a rough gravel road that virtually veered into the tide, eventually tumbling out on to a forecourt flanked by squat palm trees and gleaming white colonnades.

Emilio negotiated our first local transaction by paying the taxi drivers, and Roderick compensated on his own behalf by leading the way into the hotel. Never one to play second fiddle was Roderick, unless of course payments were involved.

"Up these steps to reception by the look of it," he announced, as if he'd morphed into a fully-armored Henry the Fifth before the breach. In the absence of valets or any other reception committee, we followed with bags under arms and carry-ons bouncing from step to step in our wake.

A rather shy girl, the owners' daughter I guessed, sat nervously behind the reception counter. The foyer, if that's what you'd call it, was clean and spacious, with wicker and leather chairs placed around a couple of round wooden coffee tables. Beyond we could see the smooth turquoise rectangle of a sizeable pool, with a phalanx of deck chairs buffeted by a faint breeze.

Such pleasant surroundings were made for hedonism, and I was not alone I'm sure in reminding myself once again that we were there for more serious purposes.

"No harm in a quick dip, do you think?" Roderick said, as if reading my thoughts. "A little relaxation could be just the thing to get us in the right frame of mind for what's to come."

Or, Roderick's subtext might have read, just the thing to get the girls into those stringy bikinis they'd bought at the quay in an effort to placate roaming vendors.

Diane sidled up to those of us at the counter with a quizzical expression.

"Have you noticed something, though?" she asked. "We're the only guests by the look of it."

She had been overheard. A young man — related to the receptionist, judging by the lean build, brunette waves and initial shyness they shared—emerged through an archway leading from the dining room.

"We had a cancellation," he said in a voice that bathed and refreshed, like warm water. "Another group comes in a few days. Until then, you are the only guests."

He was quicker to engage us than his sister had been, if indeed the receptionist was his sister, and we were won over by his smile, open and unassuming and a brilliant jewel against the golden hue of his skin. Well, let's say some of us were more won over than others.

"He's darling," Diane whispered to Greta, who grinned and raised her eyebrows as if to say *who could deny it.*

"Bit young for you," said Roderick, typically the spoiler when it came to other people's romantic aspirations.

"I wasn't thinking of running off with him," Diane hissed back. "Can't a girl just dream once in a while?"

"My name is Georgios. People call me George," our new acquaintance said in the accented English that was proving such a delight to Diane. "I'll show you to your rooms. Please follow me. We have plenty of rooms now—so one for each of you."

We left our luggage in a pile for later delivery, and followed Georgie—as Diane was now calling him—past the pool, with its chaises lounges and umbrella-shaded tables pinioned by the still-potent sun of late afternoon.

Diane advanced on Georgie at a trot, her eyes fixed on his tush. I watched her hand pat imaginary contours in his wake, and I feared the jingle of her bracelets might give her away. But Georgie didn't look back. No doubt such hazards were all part of the job.

Ahead of us was a two-story block of rooms. Like much of the rest of the hotel, it was gleaming white. Each room had a sliding French door, leading to a wooden-railed verandah for those on the top floor and a wall-enclosed patio for those down below. Scarlet and pink bougainvilleas grew around doorways and on the sides of the steps leading to the upper level. It was a very attractive façade, giving the impression of a compact village and making me feel instantly at home.

Like the others probably, all I wanted was a shower, a brief gawk at the sea, which stretched like a serene plain toward islands masked by haze, and then a nap before dinner.

We drank too much that evening and grappled with unfamiliar dishes as we talked about our expectations for the next few days.

"I thought they'd have more olives here," said Diane, and we sent Georgie scurrying off to look for some—not so much out of hunger but more to admire that limber prance of his as he relayed between our table and the kitchen.

"An Aegean Nureyev," Diane murmured with a glazed smile, and Greta and I glanced at her in bemusement. One forgets sometimes that people do change. Diane, the aloof, pouting, laconic, naive pinup so under Klara's thumb when we first encountered her, had indeed acquired a little more depth over the years or, for that matter, had perhaps been a darker horse all along than we suspected.

Besides, now that I think of it, Klara had made a point of introducing her to cultural life—an attempt to keep up with Reynard's cultivation of Anton. Ballet may well have been on the curriculum, for all I know.

It was Greta who, to no one's surprise, set the priorities for the following morning. Diane would get her chance at shop-hopping—taking into account Roderick's notion of getting a feel for the locals, and ferreting out information about Helen and her family, etcetera. Emilio and Roderick, Greta decided, would be the appropriate car renters. She and I would see what we could learn from more official channels, namely the police, and, if there were such things, local newspapers.

"An early start tomorrow, then," a rather antsy Emilio said

as a signal that it was time to call it a night. "Once we've fixed up the car rental, we can drive to the area where they found the boat. That's where I'll find the contacts my friend gave me, and it's somewhere down there where Helen's family lives too, judging from what she told me."

An unanticipated lull was affecting all of us. Here we were, on the brink of action, and we were a bit dazed by it. Travel has that effect, I've found. In transit, some find comfort in pushing away decisions that can't yet be made. Others get agitated by the wait. Now that we had arrived, procrastination had lost some of its attraction.

"Don't tell me," Roderick began scornfully after I offered my prognosis, "people can be divided into two kinds—those who revel in being on the move and those who just want to get there. It's the old dilemma, isn't it? Is the journey the point of travel, or is it the destination?"

His condescending attitude was getting to me. "Is it my imagination," I asked, "or are you getting more cynical? I don't remember you being so jaded before."

"Comes with age," he shot back.

To give him his due, Roderick was quick with an answer, albeit not always a very original one. "First impressions only come once. After that it's all repetition."

"Well, I'll say one thing," Diane joined in. "Being here like this is a first impression for me. I've never done anything like this before."

"Somebody has, though," Roderick replied. "It's all been done before by someone."

We let him have the last word. It was a difficult point to argue, especially as we didn't have a very solid grasp of what was ahead of us. But surely every search for missing persons, every floating corpse, every abandoned vessel must have something about it that hasn't been done before. Otherwise there'd be a serious shortage of whodunits.

I made short work of bedtime preparations, still feeling the effects of the wine from dinner — a slightly green-hued vintage that, to my untutored tongue, tasted oily and curiously unworthy of the spread of vegetables and shellfish it had accompanied.

There was little to ponder over in the bedroom. The décor was minimal, certainly in contrast with the classical mosaics on the walls of the dining area. The bed was a plain rectangle, and I lay in the dark looking past the open shutters at the mesmerizing luminous crescent cut into the dense indigo above. The distant swish of sea on sand and the occasional cough or creak from neighboring rooms were the only sounds.

How long I hovered on the brink of sleep I'm not sure. As I said, I was a little intoxicated and also tired from the ferry ride. So the shadowy figure who slipped through the open doorway I took at first to be a dream. Dreams can deceive the eyes, however, but they do not deceive the flesh. So it hit me in an instant that the warm skin berthing next to my own was no illusion.

I froze, trying to press my back into the mattress. The thumping of my heart and the rustle of the sheet broke into the quietness, and I was paralyzed by an unexpected excitement. With greater presence of mind, I'm sure I would have sat up at least. But my mind was drifting, and my limbs were rudderless. Even as the hand slid lightly across my stomach, I did nothing to either encourage or repel the intruder.

The hand slid lower at a glacial pace, and evidently was not put off by what it encountered, because a few minutes later I was engulfed in warm ripples ebbing up from my pelvis. All the time he — *he*, for it was definitely a male presence — was pressing against my side, until my own warmth was matched by a slick oozing down my buttock, resulting in a moist patch beneath me.

Why I just lay there like that, letting this happen, I can't explain. I suppose I was seduced. At any rate only the cadence of mumblings in a foreign accent made me stir.

"Perhaps you were looking for Diane," I whispered back. But the figure pranced out as gracefully as it had come in, departing with a kiss of my cheek and a pat on my stomach to assure me that our rendezvous, whether mistaken or not, had been satisfactory.

As so often, the present reminded me of the past. How many times had I watched Anton lie as rigid as I had been, on a couch or pile of cushions, with Reynard stroking him as if he were a collared submissive—which I suppose in effect he was—and the pungent smell of marijuana enough in itself to sap the collective will of those there gathered.

CHAPTER EIGHT

Next morning we summoned taxis for what we hoped would be a voyage of discovery back to the port. At last maybe we'd find out something significant about what had happened to our friends. We were impatient for our quest to have an end in sight.

Not that any of us were up against deadlines to be back home. In Emilio's case, he wasn't even clear whether he was going back home. It depended on what happened when he found Helen, he said. He still harbored the hope that her phone messages signaled that she'd be waiting for him with open arms.

"You've come to the right place to rescue maidens in distress," Roderick said to Emilio as the three of us shared a back seat on the coastal road. "Isn't this where they chain girls to rocks and feed them to sea monsters?"

"Not recently though," I said.

"Who knows what they've moved on to by now? Cattle prods. Electric shock treatment. Who knows?" Roderick was being his usual tactless self, and it occurred to me at that moment—call it a sixth sense if you like—that such brashness was his attempt at machismo. Perhaps he thought it was a winner with women. Reynard's successes in that arena might have pushed Roderick into developing a rival strategy.

Seen in that light, I decided, his banter became rather more amusing and less offensive than I had found it on some previous occasions.

Still, it wasn't exactly reassuring to Emilio, judging by his response: "I don't know that she's in danger of her life exactly. I'm thinking that it's more a case of her being entangled."

"With Reynard, you mean?" I asked.

"That," he nodded. "And her parents. A pretty weird couple, so I've heard."

"Didn't you say they live in a fortress?" Roderick asked.

"Well, a former fortified mansion is how Helen described it. Apart from garden walls though, I don't think there's much fortified about it now. That part of it has been crumbling away for decades. Now it's more of a country estate, I think."

As we rode, I mused silently on the visitation of the previous night. At breakfast, Georgie had made a point, I felt, of averting his eyes from me. I decided there was nothing to be gained from accosting our waiter—if indeed it had been he who had lain so tenderly by my side. Instead I decided to look back on the episode as if I had awoken from a pleasant, ephemeral dream. Appetite was satisfied. Analysis was unnecessary. Sometimes these encounters, spawned by primeval impulses, are best savored as phantasms.

Once we reached our destination, we split up on our various errands. To my mind, Greta looked irresistible in a pastel dress that very nicely bridged the gap between casual and the more business-like look we needed for our visit to the local gendarmes. Her shades, with blonde locks billowing over the lenses every now and again, were a good finishing touch. All in all, just the right blend of enticement and authority.

Unfortunately, officialdom failed to respond. I would have sworn the police officers we talked to were willfully misunderstanding us. A lack of English on their part I could understand. But when the same opaque expressions were their response to place names, our friends' names, Helen's name, her parents' names, I began to think it was more than a language barrier. None the wiser, Greta and I left for our rendezvous with the others.

We met Diane coming down one of the alleys that splayed out from the harbor. Souvenir shops flanked the flagstone path, with their wares jutting out from open facades.

In shorts, sandals, and tank top, Diane looked unapologetically touristy as she negotiated a gauntlet of baskets and paintings, miniature sculptures of Poseidon and other former movers and shakers, and the ubiquitous t-shirts.

She sauntered toward us, and my thoughts shot back, of course, to that tabloid photo of her sashaying along the King's Road. Her thighs and neck might have lost some of the tautness of youth, but she had a genetic makeup that seemed to favor eternal thinness — much to the annoyance, I would imagine, of some of her female acquaintances, and, so it appeared, much to the satisfaction of male onlookers. At least, as she passed shop owners, there was no shortage of admiring glances in her wake.

"Anything of interest?" Greta asked.

"Not really," Diane replied. "A necklace I quite liked. I may go back for it."

"Actually I was thinking more of information," Greta said.

"Oh. No. Those places we talked about are hard to remember. I did ask a couple of people, but either I pronounced the names wrong or nothing doing. They just didn't want to know."

Roderick and Emilio had been more successful in their task. They stood waiting for us at the quay, leaning on a couple of dinky little cars that looked barely capable of going up the alley we'd just walked down.

"Oh, they must have rented out all the real cars then," Diane said.

"These will get us around," Emilio said with a grin.

"And if they break down," Roderick added, "we can just carry them back to the rental office and pick up a couple more."

We squeezed into the two vehicles. Emilio and Roderick drove; Greta and I were passengers in one and Diane in the other.

"Where are you taking us, Emilio?" I asked as we revved up a slight incline heading toward the interior.

"There's a small town on the other side of the island," he said. "It's near where Helen's family lives. I have people to look up there who may be able to help us. It's in the same direction as the bays where it seems your friends and their boat were found, so we can ask some questions around there too."

Before us stretched a thin ribbon of asphalt with hardly a vehicle to be seen. In the distance, a white-washed windmill stood out like a milestone. We surveyed the bare hills with their terraces and scattering of what looked at first like intricate farm buildings. We did double takes at the turrets and decorative patterns on the walls.

"What are those?" Greta asked. "They look like miniature castles."

"Dove cotes, so I believe," Emilio replied. "The doves come in handy for dinner, although I don't think Helen was very partial to them."

Once, we stopped to stretch our legs at a ruin. A guidebook Greta had picked up in the port said it dated back to classical times. There was not much to it apart from rows of stone blocks and fragmented pavement. I forget now whether it was a temple or a villa. It could even have been a dove cote, although if the size of the place was an indication, any avian residents would have dwarfed eagles.

"Makes you wonder what they were like—I mean the people who lived here." Diane was voicing what we were all thinking, judging by our contemplative faces.

"Or whether they ever thought of us," Roderick added with a sort of giggly snort. I didn't want to give Roderick fuel for whatever absurdity he was about to express, but Diane was not so cautious.

"How could they think of *us*?" she asked.

"Not us in particular, obviously," Roderick continued. "But people in the future. You know, did they wonder whether we'd still be boating to the mainland for an oracle once in a while, or worshipping the same old gods in the same old ways, or going off on odysseys?"

"Well, we are in a way, aren't we?" Greta said. "On an odyssey."

"There you are, then," Roderick said in a tone of mock triumph. "Human urges never change. Speaking of which, I have the urge to get going again before we run out of steam and need to head back to the hotel."

The journey resumed, and just for a change I decided to join Diane in the other back seat and sample Roderick's driving for a while. Not that I didn't have some experience of his impetuous handling of a steering wheel. Roderick used to be our designated driver when he shared the house with Reynard. Back then he had a convertible—considered very cool, even in our often sodden climate. I wonder if anyone's ever done a study of how male driving techniques relate to bedroom etiquette. Probably.

The town we were going to was, inevitably, surrounded by hills, so that our first view of it was looking down on flat-roofed boxes, all gleaming white and clustered together as tightly as a rabbit warren. One, or possibly more, ocher church domes stood out above the houses, and we could pick out our route by the line of trees winding through the mass of angular buildings until it reached the arid slopes beyond.

We could see that the trees became a denser clump in the town center, and it was there that we headed, parking our cars and walking the final half mile or so until we came to a square flanked by three or four cafes. Each one had its hinterland of wooden tables and chairs, and we had our choice, because by this time in the afternoon, customers were few and far between. We chose a couple of rickety tables in the shade of a huge tree with a whitewashed trunk and swigged beer from the bottle as we gazed around at verandahs and steps leading into narrow recesses and at chalky flagstones worn, we imagined, by a millennium of walking.

"Have you noticed how everything is blue?" Diane commented. "Everything that isn't white, I mean. All the doors and window frames and railings. All the same shade, even."

"Keeps it simple." Roderick almost seemed rehearsed, as if Diane was repeating things I'd missed hearing in the car. "Besides, somebody influential probably has the blue paint concession."

He glanced at Emilio as he said it, and Emilio caught on immediately.

"Well, I don't think it's Helen's family," he said. "Now I think about it, she never actually talked about where their money came from. Just that there was quite a bit of it."

Bottle drained, Emilio sauntered off clutching a notepad listing addresses for the contacts his officer friend from the ship had given him. He'd asked inside the café for directions, and in the meantime we formulated our plans outside. We decided that while Emilio went off to see what he could find out from his sources, Roderick, Greta and Diane would squeeze into one of the cars and check out the bays where the bodies were found. I would simply stay put, which suited me fine. The beer was making me drowsy, and a little snooze in quiet surroundings was a welcome prospect.

Of course, things are never as simple as you'd like them to be. As soon as I was alone, an elderly man sat down at the next table. I closed my eyes, but he kept clearing his throat and clinking the glass he was drinking from. Eventually I straightened up with the idea of moving. He was too quick for me though.

"Tourist?" he asked. A little surprised to hear his clear enunciation, I nodded and added, "Well, not exactly."

Then I stopped. How was I going to explain in simple English what we were doing there? Sign language? Gestures? It turned out that I needn't have worried about his fluency.

"In London for six years," he continued in confident clippings. "Near Tottenham Court Road. Know it? Worked in a restaurant. Now home for me, here."

He stared at me, the way you might examine the face of a former acquaintance before committing yourself to a greeting. It occurred to me that as a local he might know something about Helen and her family. And so I asked him, and the response began with a huff.

"Not for us, that place up there," he started, and the cracks in his sallow cheeks threatened to split right through to the gums, so parched did his skin appear. Topped by a weather beaten cap and gray hair protruding like tentacles, it was a face that seemed foreign to modern times. I could visualize him as the model for a sculpture in those ruins we'd visited, except sculpture back then was all about youth and beauty and vigor. On any of those grounds this old fellow would not qualify. Then, as now, appearance was the making of a man, or woman.

Having forced his companionship upon me, the old man reminisced in fits and starts about his years in London and his youth in the vicinity of the square where we sat. Each anecdote had some tenuous link to the next, and I nodded and humphed in response until I nearly succumbed to the combination of alcohol, fatigue and that strained and rambling monotone of his. I had the feeling though that he was leading somewhere, and that if I just stayed conscious long enough I would get the point.

As he talked my eyes narrowed to slits, and the heat

induced a Vaseline-like coating of mucous so that I could hardly focus. Always in the background was the hum of his voice, as steady and unrelenting as bees in a flower bed.

I became aware then of a nebulous figure approaching across the square, and for a moment I thought I knew him. It was his way of walking, the lean physique and the swinging arms and the well-proportioned oval of the face. There are characteristics about some people that, once closely observed, always stand out.

From subconscious depths came reinforcing images. The hair was no longer shoulder-length and the clothes were more subdued in color and cut, but all the same, memories of Reynard's bedroom, the summerhouse and the parties fluttered into my head. I sat up startled, causing the raconteur opposite me to pause in mid-sentence.

"Something wrong?" he asked, his gaze following the direction of my own.

"That man," I replied. "I know him. He's an old friend. Anton."

As I said it, the approaching figure appeared to recognize me. At least, he abruptly turned ninety degrees and strode out of sight. We were like Old West gunfighters in a standoff, with one of us diving for cover.

"Must be mistake," the old man said.

"Excuse me a minute," I said, stumbling upon chair and table legs as I rose. My path across the square seemed booby trapped by an obstacle course of uneven flagstones and café furniture, but though I weaved and wavered, I was convinced of my vision. I steered straight for the gap between buildings where I'd seen that familiar profile disappear from view.

Never was the term *blind alley* more appropriate than for the crevasse I then entered. The figure might as well have been a figment. Still in a daze, I surveyed a labyrinth of narrow passageways, marble ledges and bulbous clay planters, flights of steps leading up to doorways hooded by fanlights, and everywhere that duality of dazzling white walls and blue trimmings that made me lose my bearings all the more. If it had been Anton I saw, then it was beyond any ability of mine to find him.

I returned to the table and chair where I had been sitting. The old man was gone. The waiter hovered expectantly, and I ordered another beer and resigned myself to slow sips while I awaited my friends.

An hour or more passed before I heard their chatter wafting across the square. Jolted out of my trance, I caught sight of Diane first and then the other two.

"Any news from the coast?" I asked as they joined me at my table.

"Not for the last thousand years, for the most part," Roderick said, slumping glumly over his drink.

I turned to Greta for a more lucid answer.

"No one rents boats there," she said. "There are no hire companies, nowhere around here where they could have hired a boat or a crew."

"We drove to this sleepy little fishing village," Diane added. "Apart from a hotel, there's nothing there for visitors. No facilities at all."

"Well, they got the boat from somewhere," I said. "Perhaps they got it on the mainland."

"Perhaps," said Roderick. "But then they, or someone, would have had to sail it to the island. I think that would have been a bit beyond Reynard's skills, let alone Klara's and Anton's."

Having reached this dead end, the conversation turned to me and what had been happening in the square since they'd been gone. About the old man I didn't hesitate to tell them, even about how he had left so quickly while I was on the other side of the square. The apparition of Anton was a different matter. If it really was him, why had he turned tail? I felt I may have been a little confused, what with the beer and all. Perhaps I'd tell them later.

"I hope Emilio has something more productive to tell us," Roderick said. "Otherwise we haven't got much to go on, have we?"

Greta turned to me with further explanation.

"We looked for the local police in the fishing village, but all we got were blank looks."

"It's like they just want us to leave them alone," Diane said. "We're being treated like kids. They just want us to keep quiet and let them take care of it. Well, you know, three of our friends have gone. Two drowned, maybe, although God knows where the bodies are. And the third? We don't even know who the survivor is. This is mad. It's like we've walked into some stupid film or something."

Diane's outburst stunned us. Frankly, she didn't usually stay on topic for a string of sentences that long. It showed, as if we needed to be shown, just how near our odyssey was to hitting the rocks.

To relieve the tension, I thought again about mentioning my sighting, or mirage, of Anton. Would it be false hope or fresh inspiration? It could go either way, and so I kept quiet.

Temporary relief came in the form of Emilio striding into the square. His face, with its well-defined symmetry and un-concerned glow, was well-suited to the P.R. aspects of a cruise ship officer. It was often hard to tell what he was feeling be-hind that façade.

"I don't do worry," he had told me at the hotel. "What's the point? Just deal with it and move on. That's my motto."

The exception to this was his devotion to Helen, or perhaps I should say the idea of Helen. There he did seem genuinely affected. In fact, I felt sorry for him on that score. The enigma of those phone messages she'd left, back before this trip started, was one thing he kept harping on about. He'd concocted this fable of how he was going to find her and they'd live happily ever after. In one of my less tolerant moments, I very uncharacteristically toyed with the thought of saying that maybe hers was one of the two bodies they'd found with the boat. But I just let him talk instead.

"Well," Greta asked him, "so what did your contacts tell you?"

"Very little," Emilio confessed. "They told me about the place where Helen's family lives. It's just up the road from here. But they said we'd be wasting our time to try to contact anyone. There are staff and guard dogs. You'd never get near the parents, apparently."

Greta brought Emilio up to date on the excursion to the fishing village.

"So what are we left with?" Roderick concluded. "A boat from nowhere. Bodies no one is willing to verify. A hilltop mansion we're told to steer clear of."

"We should have done more digging on the mainland — gone through official channels," Diane said. "For one thing, the consul might have given us information."

"So far I'm not very impressed with official channels," Roderick responded. "I mean the police here are behaving as if they'd like to deport us."

Shadows began to fracture the overwhelming sheen of the walls around the square. Investigating the hilltop mansion was the obvious next step, but it would have to wait. We were tired and hungry, and besides we had a deadline.

"We need to return to the hotel," Greta said. "I told Georgie we'd be there for dinner, so I don't want to let him down."

"No, we don't want to do that," Diane agreed. "We shouldn't put Georgie in a difficult position."

I waited for Roderick to add some innuendo. But he held his tongue, and we all trooped off toward the cars.

CHAPTER NINE

Dinner was a bit grim, to be honest. Our minds were not on the cuisine or the vintage, whatever it was. Once or twice I thought about giving a fuller account of what I'd seen, or thought I'd seen, in the square that afternoon. Anything, almost anything, to put some excitement back into the atmosphere.

Even Diane was in a slump. She smiled and virtually pleaded with Georgie whenever she wanted anything replenished, not her usual way at all of communicating with men she found attractive. Normally it was an icy remark or two and a purposeful lack of eye contact.

"Makes them try harder," she'd said once, in response to a reprimand from Greta about "seeming a little rude." It sounded like an attitude she'd picked up from her early days as a neophyte, although it had more of Reynard's cunning about it than the impulsive nature of Klara, Diane's primary mentor.

"If I can just find Helen," Emilio said as we re-hashed the events of the day over a final course of sorbet and fresh fruit. "That's the key. She must have left those phone messages for a reason. Something must be wrong, and the chances are your friends are somehow touched by it too."

"Well, tomorrow let's have a look at the family mansion," Roderick said. "Have we learned any more about her parents?"

"Just those parties they're known for," Emilio said, "and that's mostly speculation. Supposedly a bunch of guests in costume or masks acting bizarre. Locals won't really talk about it."

I will always remember my bedroom at that hotel, but not for any aspect of the sparse furnishings and plain walls. Its appeal centered on the rectangle of night sky that I surveyed from my bed once the French doors were pushed open and the shutters pinned back.

Calmness permeated that place to an extent that I, a city dweller, had rarely experienced. Outside, the pool and surrounding deck were chopped into still, angular shapes by the light of the moon. The white noise of the tide was the soundtrack of my wine-induced haze, that and the rustle of leaves in what remained of the day's wind.

Then, as I lay there, I heard the light slap of approaching feet on the path alongside the pool. A late-night swimmer? A light-fingered local checking for easy pickings? My restless imagination? For a minute, I froze.

An instant later and my doubts evaporated. Someone was on the patio outside my room. It was no figment. Ghosts do not scatter pebbles in their wake. Neither do their clothes scrape on branches as they creep toward the door.

I guessed whom to expect before his outline invaded my field of vision. To be honest, I was in two minds. A visitation for a second night running seemed a bit of an imposition. On the other hand, the initial experience had not been unpleasant. Much of it, as already mentioned, had merged with my dreams, so that I had woken up that morning unsure whether my passions might have been triggered by some autoerotic fantasy.

Sitting up in bed, I prepared myself to speak.

"Look, I don't think we should do this again," I was going to say. It sounded feeble even as I concocted my challenge to him. What was the harm? No one need know, and apparently it wasn't a French farce of mistaken identity, as I had suspected at first the previous night. So my gain was not Diane's loss after all. Needless to say, I hadn't breathed a word of it to her.

On the other hand, where was it leading? Did intimacy need motivation or a goal? Or could it be pure appetite, pleasurable but no more consequential than a nightcap smoothing the path to slumber? I could almost hear my pondering echoed in the voices of bygone days, those days when we friends clustered together and philosophized our desires.

What I wasn't prepared for, in my brief musing, was a second person. The silhouette was short and slender, even compared to Georgie's. For a few seconds I envisaged a ménage. Then Georgie was sitting on the edge of the bed nodding and fluttering his hand as if to reassure me.

"This is my sister," he said, and I realized I was looking at the receptionist. Such an insular young woman she had seemed behind the counter, with her downcast eyes and her dark hair braided in a businesslike twist. The prospect of a ménage, wanted or not, waned accordingly. So, if not that, what?

"I heard at dinner," Georgie continued, "how you talk about that family and their home. We, my sister and me, have been there."

Even in the shafts of half-light from outside, it was clear that Georgie's announcement was not cause for celebration on his part. His chin rested on his chest as he spoke, and I felt his hand clasp my arm for reassurance. At the foot of the bed, his sister stood as I imagined her posture might be before a priest, with head slumped over taut shoulders and hands squeezing each other. With her hair hanging loose to her breasts and a pale nightgown barely masking her form, she made an endearing figure, as if she were a supplicant or transgressor awaiting a verdict. I had the urge to put an arm around her as a comfort, but of course I didn't.

I turned back toward Georgie. If either of them were going to explain anything, it was him.

"Your friends, the three you talk about." There was a note of uncertainty in his voice, as if he was gauging whether my response was likely to be hostile or sympathetic. "They take us to that place."

"They, our friends, stayed here?" I couldn't suppress my astonishment.

"Yes," Georgie said. "They were guests."

What he told me next seemed too sordid to digest, and yet the more details he gave the more plausible it became.

"You slept with them? You and your sister?"

"Yes. The two. The man with the name Reynard and the lady. They took us to that house you talk about."

Reynard's methods were familiar enough to me that I couldn't contest what Georgie told me. How he would have relished the challenge of seducing two young foreigners. One of each gender would have been even better.

Reading between the lines, I guessed Anton had been slow to catch on to what was going on. All I could think of was that Helen, egged on by Reynard and Klara perhaps, might have persuaded Georgie and his sister to go to the house for one of those parties we'd heard about.

"We all dress up," Georgie continued, "and there is wine, and other things. After a while my sister is sleepy, and Reynard and the lady take her away to rest. She is gone a long time. She comes back. She is laughing. Then I go with them."

"They forced themselves on you?" It seemed a violation to ask, but I couldn't think at that moment how else to put it. Even as I posed the question though, I knew that it couldn't be quite that simple, and Georgie's bashful titter and barely perceptible shrug confirmed as much. Exactly how much his sister understood of this conversation I couldn't tell, but the moonlight was enough to expose a tight-lipped smile, like that of a child caught between forbidden pleasure and discovery.

"Tomorrow they want us back again," Georgie continued in a confiding whisper.

"And you will go?"

"Yes. Big party."

What hold could Reynard and the others have over Georgie and his sister to compel them to return for more of the same? I remembered Helen's parents. They were powerful people on this island. Perhaps when they wanted their way, they got it.

I thought, too, of Anton and Diane when I had first known them. There was a strange fascination about being groomed, and even exploited, by a figure of authority—a mentor, you might say. All that attention, all that praise. It was a process—a method, let's call it—that could be so mesmerizing, so irresistible in capable hands.

"You will come?"

Georgie's invitation took me by surprise.

"You want all of us to come to the party?"

For the first time, Georgie's sister showed some urgency.

"Please," she said as she stepped forward to reinforce the plea.

"For you, and us, it will be good," Georgie added.

They'd have to wait till the morning for an answer, I told them, and with a few understanding words and gestures my two visitors left.

Alone again, I feared that sleep would be slow in coming. A pillow supported me as I sat up in bed trying to sort out my feelings. The monochromatic contrast of the moonlight gave the whole episode the character of something watched on a screen or stage. Yet I knew it was real enough, and clearly it was the key to everything we did from thereon. Whatever purpose Georgie and his sister had in requesting our participation, I couldn't decide. Perhaps it was at the urging of others. Perhaps they needed allies for their own plan of escape. Or perhaps they wanted to be rid of us all, in one way or another.

Breakfast seemed as if it would never end. I could barely contain myself as Roderick and Emilio labored through plates of cooked morsels, and patience was no easier while Greta and Diane went up to the buffet table for seconds of yogurt and fruit.

The final phase of the meal—washing down the food with coffee—was what I was waiting for. This would be the right time for discussion.

Georgie had been as good as his word from the night before, that he wouldn't say anything to the others until I'd had a chance to speak to them.

As I'd expected, there was a stunned silence after I'd finished relating what had been said by my nocturnal visitors.

"So Reynard and Klara are alive?" Roderick asked at last in an incredulous tone.

"Alive," I said, "and, according to what Georgie told me, well enough to indulge in the old tricks of the boudoir."

"So whose bodies were with the boat then?" was the next question, and it came from Diane.

"Anton, you think?" Greta said.

It was time for me to reveal my supposed sighting of Anton of the previous afternoon in the square.

"It seemed like I was hallucinating," I concluded, "but I know I wasn't."

"Well, we're going, right?" Roderick jumped in. "The party, I mean. With any luck we'll kill two birds, so to speak, with one stone. We'll find out about Reynard and the others, and Emilio will locate Helen."

"It could be a bit of a shock when we turn up there," Diane

said. "I mean, if Reynard and Klara *are* there, they won't be expecting us to appear out of the blue."

"Unless Anton lets them know he saw me," I said.

"Well, didn't Georgie tell you it was a costume do?" Greta asked. "Let's wear masks. We'll just act like guests and see what happens."

"Suits me," Roderick said with a snigger. "Acting like guests sounds like it could be fun."

CHAPTER TEN

As we made our preparations that day, I found a few minutes here and there to reflect. Roderick still didn't seem entirely comfortable in the presence of Emilio, and that innate cockiness of his found frequent expression in remarks bordering on boastfulness or lasciviousness.

Fifteen years previously, when we'd all felt tribal in our closeness, his qualities seemed a bit nondescript compared to Reynard's charisma and Anton's then-blossoming persona as a bashful poet. Dark, heavy eyebrows and an equally ample head of hair had given Roderick a rather melancholy look. He wasn't especially tall or athletic. So, all in all, perhaps he'd developed wit to compensate. That, of course, and his self-perpetuated reputation for largesse in the bedroom.

Still, in present circumstances, his quickness to respond to the plight of friends in distress had to be recognized and applauded. For that matter, we'd all shown some pluck, and I'm not just saying that to pat myself on the back. For Diane and Greta too, the way they just put their normal routines on hold and ventured out to this foreign land not knowing what they'd encounter — well, that showed real devotion I thought.

Even Emilio deserved some credit for that. I mean, after the way Helen went off with Reynard, you couldn't blame him if he'd wiped those phone message of hers and forgotten about it. Exactly how devoted he was to her, bearing in mind his escapades with Greta and Diane, was still uncertain — probably to him as much as to us. But I supposed he was giving her, and himself, the benefit of the doubt. Perhaps it was another case of a sailor answering a siren's call, or in his case a trio of sirens.

In truth, I felt a little regret for not keeping in closer contact over the years. We'd been such a tight little clique, and then we'd drifted apart, what with Greta going back to Denmark and Diane getting hitched and then divorced — not that we didn't warn her about nomadic musicians.

There'd be the occasional get-together at my place or the flat that Reynard, Klara, and Anton shared. But none of the rest of us had the balls, or perhaps it was the need, to inquire more closely about what exactly their threesome consisted of. I suppose we thought if they wanted to bring it up, they would. And then came that fateful meeting, with Reynard's announcement.

As I've already said, when he started talking that day in my flat, I thought it was going to be about formalizing their relationship, perhaps through some kind of polyandry ceremony. I was not aware of anywhere on the planet where that would be legally recognized, but I could imagine Klara saying something like *If it's in the heart and it's in the loins, then it's in the stars — and that's all the recognition we need.* When Reynard told us instead about the trip they were planning, it was completely out of the blue.

Anyway, that was all brine under the bridge. Who could say now what exactly was in any of their minds? They were going on an adventure, that was about all Reynard would tell us. Well it had been that all right, and not just for them.

Armed with tips from Georgie about which shops to visit for festive apparel, we made a morning sortie into the port. The mood ricocheted between nervous anticipation about what we might discover at the party that night and a childlike excitement about getting ready for it. Apparently we weren't the first to scour the alleys for materials for masks and costumes.

In one shop in particular, we were greeted as if we were expected. The mid-fortyish couple who ran the place—husband and wife, I'd say—beamed as we entered and seemed to know exactly what sort of garments and accouterments to dig out and display. This was all the more surprising, since we weren't sure ourselves what we needed.

"Something that reveals the body but not the person," said the woman, whose command of English clearly wasn't attained locally. Bangles slid over her forearm as she smoothed fabrics with her spangled aquamarine fingernails. She had what you might call a *presence,* what with makeup and figure fit for any cosmopolitan salon.

Only when she bent over the counter did she reveal anything that didn't quite fit the lady-about-town image. As her blouse rode up over her back, I noticed a discreet tattoo, of a mermaid reposing near the base of her spine.

At the other end of the counter, the man rummaged for masks, every so often peering our way as if he was measuring us up. He had a smile from which it was hard to turn away, the whiteness of his teeth contrasting with a tan as golden as his wife's immaculately coiffured curls.

"You will look great," he enthused with emphasis. The couple stood in their doorway watching us cart away our purchases.

"Did you notice the seahorse tattoo on the man's arm?" Diane asked, a little intrigued. I hadn't, but when I looked back I noticed something else. Above the shop was a sign: *The Mermaid's Retreat.* Well, that accounted for the woman's choice of tattoo, perhaps. The seahorse? I'd have to think about where that fitted in.

With suggestions from various shopkeepers, we sorted through racks and bins across town, the search highlighting our different personalities.

Greta, for instance, went about the task as if she were

94

assembling army kit for an assault, which in a way I suppose was apt. Nonetheless, her outfit — or at least the raw materials for it — looked extremely promising. Even behind a mask, those blue eyes were as penetrating as searchlights, while Roderick was eyeing her ponytail as if he was grappling with the desire to stroke. Surely Reynard would not fail to see something familiar, even behind a disguise.

Diane was more impulsive and indulgent in the way she immersed herself in the task. Not at all like the insular Diane of old. But I've already commented on that . . .

She'd decided jewels would be the right accessory for the plain white tunic she planned to wear. We're talking about costume jewels, of course. Every so often, with much posing and fluttering of eyelashes for the rest of us, she'd try on a necklace or bracelet that sparkled enough to catch her fancy.

What's more, she decided she had to take Emilio in tow. One sight that stayed with me was of her palm resting on his bare stomach as he modeled a shirt she'd picked out. For entirely longer than seemed necessary, they stared into each other's eyes with Diane's fingernails edging ever closer to Emilio's belt. The instant only lasted a minute or two, but I couldn't help wondering what it had done to Emilio's resolve to find Helen.

Diane's moment of flirtation, that stroking of skin on skin, seemed a regression to the instincts of our youth. Like Diane's and Greta's activities with Emilio on the cruise ship, it was something of an anomaly at that point in our lives.

Since we'd reconnected with each other, our physical connections were not nearly as naïve and spontaneous as they once were. Change comes with maturity, no doubt. One becomes more cautious about the consequences of exposure, perhaps more unsure about what one has to offer — or how it will be accepted. Would a party relax our protocol in that respect, I wondered? It wouldn't be the first time.

Try to imagine a mixture of the Hellfire Club, Louis XIV's Versailles, a free concert at Hyde Park and maybe a busy day at ancient Delphi. Then throw in a few visions of the Marquis de Sade. All those comparisons were made as we invaded each other's hotel rooms, praising and occasionally mocking our various outfits.

Considering we only had that day to come up with something, we agreed we had done pretty well. Whatever kind of Bacchanalia it turned out to be, we looked prepared.

"It'll be like going to a rave, except hopefully without being totally out of our minds," said Diane, who actually had gone to various events of that sort with Klara and so had some idea what she was talking about.

Never to be outdone when it came to fleshly excesses, Roderick claimed to have gone to a free concert in Hyde Park, but "I can't remember who I heard now. So I must have had a good time."

"Let's not forget why we're going tonight," said a stern Greta, looking splendid if slightly conservative in a bronze colored mask covering her face from the lips up and a flowing turquoise dress that looked as if it might have been designed for the amphitheater on the mainland where Emilio had tried to give us the slip.

Diane and Roderick had opted for almost matching tunics that revealed a lot of thigh and chest, complemented by helmet-like headdresses crested with plumes.

Emilio, for his part, stuck with a more conventional combination of jeans and the shirt he'd bought at The Mermaid's Retreat—in addition, of course, to the mask each of us was obliged to wear.

Greta's reminder about "why we're going tonight" kept popping into my head. Georgie's revelation—that Reynard and Klara were still very much in the land of the living—plus my own sighting of Anton, called into question our entire expedition. Why *were* we going? Obviously we still wanted to find them and assure ourselves they were all right. But it now appeared that those bodies found with the boat were nothing to do with our friends. Perhaps all our time and trouble had been spent tracking down a trio of hedonists who just wanted to be left alone.

Late that afternoon I tried to nap in my room, but with these thoughts as prickly as the heat, I could only toss and turn and let my mind ramble. It was a relief when Greta called to us to assemble in the dining room for appetizers and cocktails before driving to the night's great event.

"Georgie's not leaving much to the imagination," Diane whispered to me as our waiter and his sister served us. Indeed, Georgie's costume consisted of sandals, a white loincloth and an equally unadorned vest, open at the front to show off his smooth and firm torso. His sister was clad in similar fashion, with the addition of a silver bangle and rather less exposed skin.

"Well, from what Georgie told me, his sister and he were expected to play the part of willing victims at the last event," I whispered back. "So perhaps they're dressing to look like house servants from the classical era. You know how those ancients were when it came to the hired help."

"No I don't, really," Diane said in a louder voice. "Anyway, as long as no one thinks they can take liberties with us . . ."

I couldn't guarantee that, I told her. But I wasn't too bothered. Diane had come a long way since she was Klara's trophy submissive. No one these days would take liberties without her permission.

As dusk gave way to the moon, the road ahead lay across the hills like a luminescent girdle. Emilio drove in Roderick's wake with Greta and me squeezed on to the back seat.

"What do we do when we get there?" I asked.

"Mingle," Greta replied in that firm, unhesitating tone which always implied a quiet clarity of thought. Even if she didn't know where it would lead, she never seemed to doubt her course of action. "Depends who's there I suppose."

"That might not be so easy to know, if everyone's in costume," I said.

"Well," Greta said, "all *we* need to know is whether Reynard, Klara, and Anton are there. And Helen. I suppose Emilio will be looking for *her*."

"Let's hope we don't get turned away at the door," I said. Complications seemed to occur to me so much more naturally than they did to her.

"Georgie and his sister, whatever her name is, told Diane they'd get us in," Greta answered.

Oh well, I thought, in that case why am I worrying?

In the pristine air, those arid hills could not conceal our destination once we got within a couple of miles. What time had left of the high castellated walls glowed like a beacon on its summit, their whiteness made stark and slightly intimidating by the lunar light. From within the perimeter of the fortress burst the pulsations of fire, or perhaps some artificial illuminations such as strobe.

At a distance of half a mile, the mass of the structure loomed over the surrounding olive groves with a still-vibrant power. There was a scattering of pine trees also, standing out against the sky as if they were neglected survivors of an ancient forest.

A phalanx of parked cars straddled a gravel driveway, and we joined their ranks and spilled out of our two vehicles, scrambling to don our headwear and double check our costumes. Ahead of us, inchoate figures in ornate attire drifted toward a squat stone arch in which double wooden doors had been wedged open to reveal the festivities within the walls.

Amplified music stunned us with its velocity, and forced a rise in the volume of conversation.

"Looks like there's a welcoming committee," yelled Roderick, pointing and rolling his eyes in a manner that would become de rigueur in the loud bustle of the ensuing melee.

"Helen's parents, maybe?" I shouted back. It was hard to make sense of words. Hand gestures and facial expressions were the best recourse.

Once we were out of the cars, Georgie indicated that he would go ahead with his sister. I took this to mean that he was going to make sure we received the required welcome at the entrance, and sure enough, we watched him exchange words with the couple who appeared to be the hosts. A minute later he was waving to us to approach. Whatever role Georgie and his sister played in the goings on at this place, it didn't seem to be entirely unwilling—unless their arms were being twisted in more than a literal way.

Our hosts, if that was indeed who they were, couldn't have done their job better. Their masks and the upturned collars of their flowing robes revealed little more of their faces than mouths and chins. Even so, it was enough to display smiles, followed by handshakes and hugs so spontaneous it was as if they recognized us as fast friends.

They led us under the archway, where bursts of light striated dense shadows as if we were entering a theme park or fairground attraction. It was so disorientating that Diane staggered and the male half of our welcoming committee put an arm around her waist to steady her.

As he led Diane into the courtyard beyond, his consort's turned to face us and I could swear I saw a wink behind the anonymity of her mask. But other guests were arriving, and we were obliged to move forward before I was able to take a second look.

There were perhaps a hundred people in the courtyard.

They were divided into twos and threes for the most part, with some availing themselves of marble statues for support and inspiration while others hovered in the porticos surrounding the open space. Still others slow danced in a foretaste, I imagined, of what they hoped was to come.

Costumes ranged from plain togas to animal motifs, of which goats, donkeys and horses were the most abundant. These motifs were favored particularly by the menfolk, of course, giving wearers the opportunity to indulge in priapismic excesses shared with hilarity and, in some cases I swear, a degree of envy that seemed absurd, considering they were mostly the stuff of wishful thinking.

Female attire was more colorful although not necessarily more tasteful. Breasts not yet bared were promoted by plunging necklines and a degree of uplift that might have warranted red faces had they not all been masked.

Among those with less pronounced figures, the nymph look was in vogue, with flowing hair crowned by floral wreaths. One or two blew on flutes while their sisters clung to anything male and fingered the more supple instruments vaunted by their escorts. Very fetching it was as we witnessed these unleashed libidos, and with an obvious appeal to those men, mostly older ones, who had still to attract partners. The temptation to fondle such nubile bottoms without fear of legal consequences was irresistible to not a few.

Our eyes were drawn to one cluster in particular, in which a couple of men were supporting a woman with her legs wrapped around the hips of a Minotaur-like statue, and with her hands clutching the statue's horns like a white-knuckled rider on a roller coaster. Every few undulations she rose just enough for us to see a length of jutting marble emerge from her crotch. Nonchalance does not come easily on such occasions, but rather than look like novices we tried our best.

Georgie and his sister were no longer to be seen, and Emilio had gone off to scout around for Helen. Greta, Roderick and I wandered over toward Diane and the still attentive host. The two of them were standing on the edge of the only sizeable group in the courtyard. A couple of dozen people were standing in a semi-circle, as onlookers do when they encounter a street performer or a fight.

Diane and her escort were wasting no time getting familiar with each other, judging by the proximity of his lips to her ear lobe. But perhaps that was a hasty conclusion. The tribal tempo ricocheting around the courtyard prohibited normal conversation. Volume, as much as desire, made a necessity of close encounters.

That was certainly the case when our hostess from the entrance rejoined us. I could feel her breath on my cheek and her fingers tighten around my wrist as she half-deafened me with a bellow.

"I do like to see my husband enjoying himself," is what I think she said.

She pushed through the crowd until she was able to put an arm over her husband's shoulder and kiss him. It's an odd thing to see masked faces locking lips, and odder too, I would shortly realize, to see masked beings indulging in full body contact. I was left to fill in the expressions and exclamations hidden behind the masks and the music, as if this was a game with missing pieces that had to be imagined.

The couple moved forward to the center of the circle, and I became aware that the crowd was focused on a naked woman strapped to a wooden trestle. It was an ancient artifact by the look of it, well in keeping with the martial history of its surroundings, and yet a reminder to me of one of those padded gym horses over which I had to do the splits at school.

At any rate, the young lady was bent over it with her ankles secured so that her legs were astride and her chin rested on the padded cylinder topping the trestle. In this position, even with her dark hair bundled into a sort of bun, she was unable to see her hind quarters or resist any advance upon them.

Husband and wife stood in front of this helpless target and, responding to cries and wolf whistles from the onlookers, the wife shed her cloak and reached with what seemed like practiced glee into her husband's pants. Unzipping with one hand, she gave an affectionate squeeze to the rigid contents with the other. It didn't take much imagination to realize that the buttocks exposed alongside the trestle were the intended destination.

But then, during a break in the music, the wife suddenly released her hold and, gesturing toward the tethered limbs spread before them, said in a loud voice: "This one is for later."

There was a collective groan of disappointment, and I heard smatterings of languages with which I was barely acquainted — French, German, Spanish, Esperanto perhaps, and other tongues I couldn't begin to fathom. Well, I could get the gist. Lust spurned is probably universal. And there were a few choice words in English of course — although heavily accented.

The wife knelt to pick up her cloak and threw it over the young woman, leaving just the head uncovered. As she did this, I noticed a mark on the wife's back, a skin blemish perhaps. The shape caught my attention, though, and I stepped forward for a closer look. What I then saw was the tattoo of a mermaid.

CHAPTER ELEVEN

We ambled into a corner of the courtyard, enticed by a bartender and waitress—clad in what might pass for the scanty garb of classical era servants. Diane had sauntered back to join Greta and me. Roderick had advanced to take a closer look at the manacled woman who, despite being put on hold, so to speak, was still drawing a crowd.

"So what did your escort say to you?" I asked Diane as we sampled from a tray of wine. Dialogue was, by this time, no longer a matter of mime and maximum volume. The music had reverted to a pastoral ditty accompanied by acoustic guitar strums, recorded bird calls, and electronically generated effects that panned between the speakers.

"Oh, just that I was free to do whatever I wanted," she replied, alternating between bites of baklava and gulps of a ruby vintage. "I'm not sure I'm ready to be stretched over a barrel or whatever yet, though. Perhaps after a couple more glasses . . . My, this is potent stuff, isn't it."

I told them about catching sight of the mermaid tattoo, which led Greta to ponder over who exactly the hosts were at this event.

"I just thought those two were Helen's parents when we came in," Diane said.

"So if they're not, which ones are Helen's parents?" Greta asked.

We scanned the courtyard rather languidly, as if we expected a couple to suddenly rip off their masks and yell, "It's us!" What we did notice, however, was that Mrs. Mermaid, as we began calling her, had taken quite a shine to Roderick. Greta was the first to see it, and spoke up with uncharacteristic gusto.

"It looks as if those two have paired off," she said. "Just hope her husband doesn't get upset about it."

"What, Mr. Seahorse? Doubt if he will," Diane said. "That's part of what he was talking to me about. *This is a free-for-all* is more or less what he said. Anything goes. With anyone's spouse or partner or whatever."

"Chances are you wouldn't even know who it is you're with anyway — what with the masks and costumes and all," I added.

Whether Roderick knew he had a free pass to pleasure, I couldn't say. He certainly didn't seem to be bothered by the fact that Mrs. Mermaid and Mr. Seahorse were nudging him into a shadowy section of a colonnade. Seahorse was doing most of the talking, punctuating what he was saying with guffaws and touchy-feely stuff. His wife was making whatever passed in this scenario for bedroom eyes, with one hand on Roderick's chest and the other smoothing the seat of his tunic.

At the time it didn't cross my mind that the wine and hors d'oeuvres played a strong part in these proceedings. Later though, it dawned on me. Whatever the concoction was, I realized, it must have affected our behavior that night.

Even after the first glass, it had been evident that the wine generated a particularly strong buzz, while I never did succeed in working out what was in the hors d'oeuvres. Roderick's surrender to temptation was an indication of this potency, but hardly cause for scandal. It wasn't as if this was his maiden ménage.

No, far more striking — disturbing, one might even say — was the effect on Greta. Up to then, she had been the one keeping us firmly on compass point. Roderick or even Diane might get distracted from our task, but Greta's mind was pinned on finding out what had happened to Reynard, Klara, and Anton. She was our pilgrim, making progress despite the lure of loud music, strong drink, and naked bodies.

Perhaps such a buffet of temptations was too much even for her. At any rate, she began to take an aberrant interest in Georgie, who was standing rather glumly on the edge of the crowd.

"He looks so vulnerable, doesn't he," Greta said with a confusing mixture of maternal concern and cougarish lust. It was a dissonance I'd have expected from Klara at her Geminian best, but hardly from the fiord-cool Greta. Or were fiords further north than Denmark? Geography was never my forte.

To add to the tension of the moment, I was half convinced that Diane scowled in response to Greta's observation. After all, it had been Diane who had taken a shine to Georgie at the hotel. And for that matter, it had been me he had visited in the middle of the night. Jealousy is not big on my agenda, though. I was content to leave Greta and Diane to make any moves on our little waiter turned temple slave or whatever he was dressed to be.

A move was not long in coming. Greta weaved toward Georgie and, sliding her arm through his, drew him toward a doorway which led out of the courtyard into some inner sanctum we had yet to explore.

"Come on," Diane said to me. "I think we need to keep an eye on her."

It was extraordinary, really, how Greta changed in the twinkling—make that *twinkle*—of an eye. Georgie couldn't help succumbing. You could see it in his expression. Whereas young women, in classic literature anyway, have that demeanor of dread or bewitchment as they are being led off for illicit purposes by a more experienced member of the opposite gender, young men under similar circumstances look positively ecstatic—from what I know of it, anyway. There's that mixture of anticipation and disbelief in their faces. Paradise awaits, they must be thinking. Makes them such easy prey. No wonder relatively few older women consider the chase worth the bother

In Greta's case, the approach was as much body language as anything she said. As usual, she was a little taciturn, something I attributed in part to self-consciousness about English not being her first language—although she could speak it as well as I could. Her dress clung to her body, giving each undulating step the flow of a slow dance. At the same time, her arm lassoed Georgie's waist so that they were virtually joined at the hip.

Goes to show, I suppose, that you never really know people as well as you think. Or maybe it goes to show that under the right circumstances, any of us will do anything.

We threaded through the crowd milling around the trestle, the victim still stretched across the frame for all to admire or investigate. Mrs. Mermaid's cloak had been removed, and an emerging round moon added its glow to the young woman's luminous skin.

As we reached the far side I felt Diane's hand clasp my wrist.

"Did you see who that was?" she asked, staring at me with wide eyes. "Georgie's sister."

"Tied up on that piece of furniture or whatever it is?" I asked.

"Yeah. I caught a glimpse of her face."

"It's hard to make out who she is with that gag in her mouth," I said, "but I thought I recognized the hair." There were plenty of youthful brunettes in this part of the world, from what I'd seen, but there was something extra luxuriant about Georgie's sister's tresses. Plus she was quite adept at braiding, a skill I'd silently admired at close quarters during her bedroom visit. The embellishment was clearly a point of pride, and not easily overlooked.

"Just adds to the confusion, doesn't it?" I continued. "I mean, how do you decide who's willing and who isn't, let alone who's dead and who isn't? Perhaps she likes being restrained. Some people do, you know."

By that time Mermaid and Seahorse were well out of the picture, their place beside Georgie's sister being taken by a man whose grey body hair and thick accent indicated that he was, in this order, late middle aged and German. He clearly relished the sight of a naked young lady stretched and secured in such a helpless fashion, and began lightly scouring her buttock and back with a small whip.

"Nothing like a perfect stranger to stimulate the nerves," he observed to us, apparently taking us to be her friends or guardians. "Such punishments should be anonymous, don't you think? So much more exciting for all concerned."

As we hurried away he had moved on to inserting fingers into orifices. From the resulting moans, it was hard to tell whether Georgie's sister reciprocated his views or not.

Diane and I followed our quarry down stone steps to a cellar. We stood just outside the doorway and watched Greta back Georgie into a recess in the wall. Shadow reduced the two figures to vague shapes, with Georgie merging with Greta's dress like cumulus ghosting across a deep blue sky.

We had to rely on Greta's murmurs, echoing through the bare room in restive bursts, for what was going on between them.

"That's it. Your finger feels divine. Like that . . . Mmm, you're making me wet. Can you feel it? Inside. Go on."

Her words were spliced with the sputter of lips on skin and the tremulous response of a young man's breathing. Without a clear view, I was forced to rely on imagination, and that in turn brought to mind a scenario from years previous. Funny how those mental associations work, isn't it.

Back then, in this scenario anyway, it had been Anton rather than Georgie who had been the leading man. It had been a rather languorous Sunday afternoon at Reynard and Roderick's rental. The usual crowd was milling around the summerhouse, and Reynard, Greta, Anton and I were smoking a joint in one of the upstairs bedrooms.

Suddenly Reynard announced that he wanted to wrestle with Anton. At first Anton shrugged it off. Bashful as he was, he evidently couldn't see why Reynard would want to stage a wrestling match in front of Greta. I can't remember now whether she was still engaged to Reynard, but anyway it seemed an unseemly thing to do.

Reynard insisted, though, and so Anton and he started grappling on one of the beds. There was much rubbing together of pelvises and twining of limbs around limbs, the kind of thing that makes some of us ponder on the erotic component in male fighting games in general.

Now Anton may have had a lean frame and a rather submissive personality at that point, but he was no pushover when it came to tests of strength. Masculine pride began to assert itself in him, and after the two rolled around for a while it was Anton who emerged on top.

Thinking about it later, I wondered whether Reynard had planned it that way. Alternatively, it could have been just the opposite of what he wanted. He was such a control freak. His intentions could be so devious when it came to power exchanges.

At any rate, Reynard was forced to concede the contest and, on being freed, announced that he was going downstairs to have a bath.

I drifted into the hall outside, but I could still see and hear what was going on in the bedroom. For the longest time, in fact, neither Anton or Greta stirred. But then Greta spoke in a soft, matter-of-fact tone, as if she had been holding back on the rules of the match.

"I think he expects us to go to bed," she said. It was as if she was conscious that she was intended as the winner's prize. But Anton's head was still bent over his chest and he was gazing at anything but her. And, of course, he didn't say a word.

A long, long time later Anton and I were reminiscing and that episode came up.

"Do you think what she said was an invitation?" he asked me. "I didn't know how to deal with it. If she'd just made a move . . . Story of my life. Watching and waiting."

Not this time, though. With Georgie, that is. Greta was making her move all right. In fact, it was a blessing in a way that it was so dark in that cellar. I could just picture the irritation on Diane's face. Picturing it was enough. I didn't want to have to actually see it. Oh well, Diane had her chance.

Appropriately, it was our latest recruit who interrupted further contemplation.

"There you are," came the voice behind Diane and me. I was so far into daydreams his sudden arrival was quite startling.

"Emilio," I whispered. "Where have you been? We lost sight of you. Did you find Helen?"

For a moment, Emilio stared into the gloom without answering, but I don't think he could make out whom he was seeing in the love clutch in the corner. There were so many couples and trios and quartets in the shadows of that complex that after a while you just lost interest in who most of them might be. You just watched their moves, and empathized with their passions.

"No," he said at last, "but I did find someone else."

CHAPTER TWELVE

So it was that Diane and I left Greta to acquaint Georgie with the ways of older women and filed back into the courtyard.

"You're quite sure it was him?" I asked Emilio as we followed. He'd left the details somewhat vague, but there weren't too many individuals we were interested in. And if it wasn't Helen he'd found, then who else could it be but one of our errant friends?

"Not entirely," he said, "but even if you can't see their faces, people have ways of moving and standing that you remember sometimes. And I had a lot of time to look at them when they were on the ship with Helen."

Emilio led us into an annex where yet another crowd mingled around a spectacle buried in its midst. Torches burned kerosene, or something similar, and the flames converted onlookers into a shadow theatre projected on to stone walls.

"In here you saw him?" Diane had to raise her voice as we neared the excitement.

"Yeah," Emilio confirmed. "He was standing, as if he was some sort of sentinel. He was next to a woman."

"Not Helen, apparently?" I said, rashly hoping that perhaps we could wrap up two missing person reports in one go. Of course he'd already said he'd drawn a blank on her, but optimism flows as freely as wine at a time like this.

Emilio looked affronted, which I didn't quite understand at that moment.

"I don't think so," he said. "I couldn't really see her. She was, well, squatting."

"Squatting?" I repeated.

"Yeah, you know, on top like."

"On top?" Diane was as much in need of clarification as I was.

Then suddenly we realized what he meant. We'd edged into the throng by this time and could see what all the fuss was about. On a low platform covered by a rug lay a man with his head pointing toward us. A woman sat astride his pelvis, her hips gyrating, her fingers kneading her scalp and then compressing her breasts with such energy that, even though she wore a mask, it left no doubt that she was highly aroused.

This impression was reinforced by what I could see of her face, that being mainly confined to a gaping mouth and a tongue perpetually circling her well-lacquered lips. Her chin and jaw line, and even her breasts, had a peculiar pallor which accentuated the unearthly, almost supernatural, effect she had on proceedings. After a minute of staring, I realized that she was adorned with a chalky paint of some kind. It certainly added to the sense that she was somehow elevated in her passions, and in her authority to exercise them. At any rate, spectators and attendants deferred to her every whim.

The man lay stretched beneath her, his movement limited to spasms so constrained that one almost swore he was bonded to the ground. Firm and rounded muscles defined his chest and upper arms, dark even in the glow from the torches.

If the volume from her audience had allowed, the moans and gasps from these two main participants would surely have been enough to summon the underworld. In fact, looking at the costumes around me, I could have been convinced that the underworld had already arrived.

What struck me most, though, was the woman's posture. In the arch of her spine, her splayed thighs, the thrust of her breasts, there was a boldness, an exercise of rights you might call it, that seemed almost contrary to the normal order of things — the normal order of things, as it occurred to me at that moment, being males as the assertive or more active gender, at least when they're in the grip of intimacy.

Well, why should I think that? After all the adventures I'd had with Reynard and friends over the years, you'd think I'd know better than to expect females to restrict themselves to passive roles. Not that there's anything wrong with submissive or passive roles. Lying on your back and letting it happen does have its transcendental benefits at times.

Diane was virtually paralyzed by the display before us. Had she been nude and slightly paler, she could have passed for one of the marble statues strewn around that property. Any hope of diverting her attention back to our main purpose looked slim.

As we watched, there was a pronounced shudder from the man, and in response the woman raised herself off her haunches with a dexterity that seemed almost unhuman. I was reminded of things I'd read about the relationships between gods and mortals in ancient times. The way the gods just had their way and there was nothing you could do to stop them. There was that sort of potency in what I was seeing.

The man rolled to one side of the platform and, as he started to get to his feet, a hitherto undetected figure emerged from an alcove behind him. It was hard to make out much about this figure, other than that he was directing the action like a master of ceremonies.

He was male. His bare chest revealed that. But, as with so many others in that gathering, further revelations were restricted by the details of costume. In his case, this consisted of a couple of skins — of goats, I would guess, judging by the curling horns that crested his head.

In any case, one of these skins served as a mantle over his shoulders and the other as a loincloth. He stepped up to the woman in a rather regal pose with arms folded, and the two of them talked guardedly to each other while scanning the crowd.

As she gave a nod in our direction, my skin tingled — the way it might have done in a long ago class when a teacher demanded an answer I was still brooding over. I braced myself, unsure what would be required of the chosen one. But when one of the couple's minions stepped into the crowd it was not me he selected. It was Emilio he gripped by the arm and led toward the platform.

At first our companion resisted with a passive, lead-footed dawdle, at the same time mouthing limp protests. *No, not me. Please, someone else.* But those around us seemed to thrive on his discomfort and pushed him forward. *Yes, go on. You're the one.* It's amazing how much pleasure a crowd can take in an individual's plight. Quite disturbing, actually.

To begin with, the woman merely linked her arms around Emilio's neck and, to the cheers of onlookers, kissed him with an ardor suggesting a deep penetration of her tongue. As she drew back, he turned his head as if searching faces for Diane or me. Even with the impediment of the mask, his expression seemed to be noticeably wide-eyed. At first I put it down to the forcefulness of his suitor. Later, when I knew more, I wondered if he recognized something about her which I had not yet grasped.

The woman knelt in front of him and probed with burnished nails at his groin. It would have taken an exceptionally willful being to resist, and so Emilio's gradual descent to a prone position and her triumphant mounting of him seemed almost a foregone conclusion.

The audience for this was by now thoroughly intrigued, and I must admit I was no different. I wasn't yelling encouragement, as some nearby men were, but I was definitely engrossed. It jolted me then when Diane tapped me urgently on the shoulder.

"Notice the nails?" she said in a cross between a whisper and a gasp. Until she clarified the remark, my first thought was some sort of ritual crucifixion was in the offing.

"Her nails," Diane stressed. "Don't you see, when the light strikes them right? They have a purple sheen to them, I swear."

I strained to get a good look, but half of what I was seeing was probably a figment of my imagination anyway.

"So what?" I responded somewhat blankly.

"Well, that together with the hair," Diane said, her tone getting more insistent. "Surely you noticed the hair? The color, I mean."

I have to admit, I hadn't really. There was so much to take in. Diane had to say her name before I got it.

"Klara?" I repeated. I stared with fresh purpose. Diane would know better than most. After all, she'd been a lot more intimate with those nails and that hair than most.

"I think you could be right," I said. What to do about it, though, I couldn't decide.

"Maybe there'll be an interval," I said rather lamely, "and we can go up and introduce ourselves."

"Introduce ourselves?" Diane repeated with scorn.

"Well, you know. Like Stanley."

"Stanley who?"

"The *Doctor Livingston, I presume* Stanley."

"Hardly," Diane said. "It's going to be more like *What the hell is going on here? We've come halfway around the planet because we thought you were dead. Couldn't you have let us know what was going on?*"

To say she was upset would be an understatement. In other circumstances, Diane and her outburst that would have been the center of attention. But Klara, if it was truly her, was still having too much fun with Emilio's body to relinquish the spotlight.

Male humiliation seemed to be part of the objective on the

platform. Well, perhaps that was just a byproduct of female resilience, or at least this particular female's capacity to out-last several partners. In each case, the guy in the goatskin stepped forward to hustle the deflated male back into the au-dience. Then another sacrificial victim was selected, and the process repeated itself with the same pelvic squats from the female and the inevitable shudder and collapse from the male.

In this fashion, Emilio returned to us. Diane smiled sympa-thetically at him, no doubt trying to show that not all females have the nature of tarantulas. But actually, Emilio seemed lit-tle the worse for violation, and the healing process was aided by comradely slaps on the back and chuckles from men in the crowd.

He grinned at Diane as he passed through this gauntlet, and she asked him, "Are you all right?"

"A little battered and bruised," he said with a note of bash-fulness, like a youth might after being ceremonially pum-meled in a gang initiation. Indeed, the furrows on his chest left by female nails were beginning to welt, and perhaps even he was unmindful of his fingers rubbing his groin where the action had been.

Suddenly he stood straighter and his attention returned to the platform.

"There. Do you see him?" he said with some urgency.

"Lord Goat, you mean?" Diane asked.

"No . . . although there is something about him that rings a bell. No, I mean the fellow behind him."

I re-focused on the shadowy presence hovering behind the main action, and when I realized what, or rather whom, I was seeing, I felt a heated quiver reminiscent of the kind that women complain about in late middle age. It was indeed the same supple form that had darted away from me in that little town square where I had sat with my drink listening to an old man's anecdotes about his barely-recalled life in London.

As had been the case with Klara, a mask and costume could not hide an identity that had once been so familiar to us.

"You're right," I said, looking at Diane for confirmation. "It's Anton, I'm sure of it."

Diane was still fixated on the platform, where yet another male was writhing in the scissor grip of female thighs. I thought of the African savannah, as seen on TV, with the antelope in a doomed struggle against the lethal grace of the cheetah. What Diane was thinking of I'm not sure, but I suspect there was a little nostalgia there. She had, after all, some experience of the compulsive joys of that conflation.

"Come on," I said. "We have to catch up with Anton and find out what's going on. That's what we're here for, after all."

With Emilio in tow, I took a firm hold on Diane's wrist and led her through the throng toward Anton, who by this time was drifting away from the platform.

As we got nearer, I raised my voice to him. "Anton. Anton, is that you?"

I wasn't altogether surprised when he hurried away from us, because I'd already been through that once with him. It was a little exasperating to be treated that way by a friend. But we'd come a long way for a friendship, and I wasn't about to give up. At the very least, I wanted to know why he was trying so hard to avoid us.

He began to run, and we followed. I had loosed Diane by this time, and she was calling after him. But he wouldn't stop. We jogged across an Italianate garden, all oblongs and jutting neatly clipped evergreens. Our quarry showed no sign of accepting capture. Emilio, it's true, probably could have bounded ahead and caught up with him. There was still the expectation though that surely Anton would stop trying to elude us and would talk.

Among the shadows cast by statues and shrubbery, we lost

sight of Anton once or twice. But we kept up the chase until it led us to a perimeter wall, and a wrought iron gate shuddering with the force of having just been flung open. Beyond was the parking area, and we emerged into it in time to see Anton vaulting into the passenger seat of a convertible. Further pursuit was pointless, and we watched the driver as she backtracked on the gravel road and accelerated out of sight with her passenger, now maskless, sneaking glances to the rear.

All three of us must have looked crestfallen as we stood there panting and staring into the night. But Emilio seemed excessively agitated.

"That was Helen driving," he said, his pitch wavering with the surprise of it. "Why, on earth . . ."

I let Emilio's voice trail off before adding a question of my own.

"Where do you think they're going?"

"Perhaps we should drive after them," Diane said. "There's only one road. Perhaps we'd find them."

"It's worth a try," I agreed. "But first of all we need to go and find Greta and Roderick. We can't drive off and abandon them here . . . although I have a feeling Roderick at least would be able to get a lift back to the port, if not the hotel."

In the courtyard people had dispersed toward peripheral rooms, and on our approach, we had a largely unobstructed view of the flagstone expanse where we had last seen Roderick being hustled off between Madame Mermaid and her consort with the seahorse tattoo.

Georgie's sister had been transferred to another device, apparently without complaint. She now hung spread-eagled in a vertical frame. It looked like an upended bed, minus the mattress and springs. Her wrists and ankles were secured by metal bands attached to ropes and pulleys, so that any movement of her ankles or wrists initiated a mechanism whereby a dildo was launched into her vagina. Only by remaining motionless could she prevent this. But of course passersby were doing their best to keep her mobile. Her hair had been rearranged from a bun to a ponytail, and there weren't many males who could resist an agitating tug to get the ropes working. A few females too, for that matter.

Feathers to the soles of her feet were another favorite, as were a pinch of a nipple and the light swish of a cane on her buttocks. Other admirers stood back in a congregation, gazing as the bands glinted around those delicate wrists and ankles, chuckling at the sleek projectile pushing into her.

What she thought about this was hard to ascertain, considering the ball gag in her mouth. Apparently, the gag was a semi-permanent fixture, at this venue at least. One thing for sure though—even in the lapses between external stimulation, she was writhing enough to keep that dildo in almost continuous motion. Where there's a will, it seems, there's a way.

At one point the frame was lowered into a horizontal position, so that Georgie's sister was lying face-up on a slab of stone. The gag was removed and a blindfold added. This episode must have been pre-arranged, or perhaps a replay from past events. People flocked around in anticipation. For a minute the nature of these rites was a mystery to me. Then the crowd parted to allow the bartender and waitress to step forward bearing bowls.

First the waitress poured honey over the length of Georgie's sister's nakedness, from her brow to her toes. The gilded liquid coagulated into puddles in hollows and crevasses and trickled in streams over smooth, rounded flesh. Next was the turn of the bartender, who added a splash of wine to the mix. Then came a final topping of grapes and raisins scattered over the body of the faintly moaning subject.

As the waitress and bartender stepped back, the crowd moved forward. Suddenly Georgie's sister disappeared beneath a frenzy of bobbing heads. Every minute or so, a mouth would emerge from the melee with lips coated in a burgundy paste and tongue stretching for globules on nose and cheek. No sooner did one head come up for air than another filled its place, until there was a sated ring of laughter around the victim. As the concoction was consumed, participants were reduced to licking the remnants off each other. Then Georgie's sister, still gasping and wriggling, surfaced again in the midst of the parting throng. And once more the dripping frame was raised, like a picture positioned for pleasure.

As we took all this in, Georgie wandered over. He looked a little embarrassed about his sister's predicament.

"Every time we come here, this is what they want her to do," he said, his broken English further fragmented by discomfort.

"They've done this to her before?" I asked, not quite sure who *they* were.

"Yeah. But it's okay."

Apparently, for Georgie at least, it was. Muttering something about finding Greta, he went back from whence he had come.

"I'm not sure it would be okay with me," Diane said with a nod of her head at the suspended sister.

"I can sort of see it," Emilio said, sounding like Roderick's echo. "Kind of freeing in a way. There's something uplifting about it, don't you think? Giving yourself like that, sublimating the ego and all that."

With the girl's skin emitting an ochre glow in the light of torches and her hair shimmering in response to each thrust of the dildo, there was an aesthetic appeal to the scene, I had to admit. In certain circles, it might well have passed for performance art and qualified for highbrow critiques and substantial financial compensation. It all depends on the labeling, doesn't it?

Still, Diane looked at Emilio for a few seconds as if she was taken aback that he would have voiced such an idea.

"A man *would* think like that," she said. It didn't ring with conviction though. It sounded like one of those throwaway lines people utter when they're not quite sure whether they want to reveal their true feelings.

Over by an arcade, Georgie was beckoning to us. Greta was just beyond him, perhaps in more ways than one. She was back to the aloof posture more typical of her, and Georgie was acting more like a servant than a victim of seduction. The more he hovered and tried to impress her with smiles and comments, the less attention she paid. Not that we could hear what he was saying, but evidently even with the aid of gestures, it didn't seem of sufficient importance to Greta.

"The effects of the wine must have worn off quickly," was Diane's acerbic observation. "Greta always did have a short recovery period."

Not as short as Klara's, based on current evidence, I was tempted to say, but I didn't. Between Klara's exhibition on the platform and Greta's abduction of Georgie, Diane's state of mind might have been too fragile to cope with any attempt at humor.

When we reached her, Greta seemed to be absorbed in the goings on in a small room attached to the arcade. We joined her in silent contemplation of Roderick and his still very attentive escorts, Mermaid and Seahorse. All three naked bodies were immersed in a luxuriant pile of cushions, and apparently under the spell of wine. I say this because Roderick appeared to be oblivious both to his audience and to Seahorse's face nuzzling up against his pelvis. Just how favorably Roderick was responding to this affection I couldn't say, my view of his mood indicator, as it were, being blocked by the aforementioned visage.

I can speak with more authority, however, about activities at his other extremity. There were still some remnants of hors d'oeuvres on a low table on the far side of the cushions. Roderick plucked a couple of grapes from a stem and, to chortles from both parties directly affected, inserted them into the subterranean recesses of Mrs. Mermaid, whose legs were strategically placed around his torso in anticipation of such a maneuver. It wasn't an entire surprise to me, and I suspect neither to Greta and Diane, when Roderick next endeavored to remove the said fruit with his tongue.

It took several minutes to accomplish this. No doubt the job could have been done quicker, but with Mermaid's fingers stroking his hair and her grunts resonating in his ears Roderick must have been under the impression that speed was not of the essence.

Rather more unanticipated was his next move. Buoyed perhaps by his success with the grapes, Roderick delicately picked up a slab of baklava and attempted an encore along the same lines.

A tasty morsel indeed was that baklava, based on earlier samples in the courtyard. But by its nature it does not insert readily. Indeed that might well have been a deliberate calculation on Roderick's part, for no one who witnessed the episode can doubt the satisfaction obtained from his prolonged cleansing of Mermaid's intimate parts.

Both Roderick and Seahorse were most thorough in their activities, and Mermaid would have been stretched, so to speak, to detect the slightest gastronomic smear or aroma in the wake of Roderick's tongue.

All of us, even the hard-to-impress Greta, were content to watch this procedure until completion. Any notion of interruptus seemed cruel and unnecessary in view of the obvious delight of those most closely involved.

Eventually the bodies rolled apart, and we were able to

catch Roderick's attention.

"What's been going on?" he asked as he swayed up to us. Apart from an askew mask he was naked, and his skin glistened as a result of his recent exertion.

"Quite a lot, actually," Diane said in the edgy tone of someone who had made a tennis court reservation too late and had to watch from the sideline. "We've found Anton and Klara."

"You have? What about Reynard?"

"Still a bit of a puzzle, he is," I said. "But the problem is Anton doesn't want to talk to us."

"He doesn't?" Roderick echoed. "I'll make him talk. After coming all this way . . ."

"Well, first of all you'd have to catch up with him." This was Emilio's first utterance for a while, what with the strain of his personal involvement in the proceedings and then the drama he'd just witnessed as a spectator.

"He always was a bit of a wriggler, our Anton, wasn't he?" Roderick said. He had never taken to Anton the way Reynard did. Saw him as the upstart rival for Reynard's affection, I shouldn't wonder, although anyone remotely close to Reynard would have to accept that upstarting was par for that particular course.

Anyway, I felt I had to say something in Anton's defense. "That's not entirely fair. Elusive is more the word, I think."

"Elusive?" Roderick wasn't exactly being hostile. It was more like he was channeling one of those celebrity toast events where the victim gets skewered oh so affectionately and the grudges get sucked in for future reference.

"As I recall," he continued, "Anton wasn't so much elusive as an adept at playing hard to get. For all but Reynard, anyway."

Diane joined in. Apparently we were tapping into some long buried feelings here.

"But when he *was* got," she said with a mirthful gurgle that was hard to interpret as either approving or otherwise. "He played as hard as anyone."

"True," Roderick conceded. Being Roderick though, he couldn't resist dragging out the topic in hopes of the last word.

"Played hard with Reynard, you might say, after he got into the spirit of it. But playing hard doesn't necessary mean being assertive. As a matter of a fact he seemed quite passive, from what I remember. Just lay there and let Reynard have his way."

I really needed to speak up. Fashionably androgynous as Anton was when we first knew him, it did tend to give the impression that he had a soft center. But there was more backbone to him than he readily revealed. Perhaps that reticence was to his detriment.

Upbringing must have had a lot to do with it in his case. When he knew me better and felt he could confide, he told me how he'd been brought up to bottle up feelings. Those years in boarding school must have contributed, what with the threat of the housemaster's cane and routine bullying from the older boys. Who knows what punishment meant to him? Keeping it inside might become a point of honor after experiences like that.

All the same, perhaps if he'd have just spoken out more with Reynard and Klara, vented his true feelings, everything might have turned out differently.

"I don't think you fully understand Anton," I said as Roderick gaped with skepticism. Why I decided this was the moment to give the argument for the defense I couldn't tell you.

"I don't know how it stands now," I went on, "but when he first began hanging out with us, it was actually Klara he was fixated on. You may have forgotten that. He was so shy around women he couldn't think of any way of being near her except through Reynard. It's not that he wasn't genuinely fond of Reynard, but there was stuff he wouldn't have gone along with if he hadn't felt so strongly about Klara."

"So how come you have these insights?" Roderick asked.

"After a while he started telling me things," I said. "But it didn't come easily to him. As I say, he might feel differently now."

"Well, the three of them are still together," Diane said, "or were anyway — before this jaunt."

"Well, yeah," I said. "But we might be reading too much into that. There were a few years where I think we all were slipping in and out of touch with each other, weren't we?"

Absorbing as these thoughts were to most of us, we became aware that one of our number was not so engrossed. Emilio was staring in the direction of the parking area.

"I think we should go after Anton and Helen," he said, adding with a slightly derisive twist, "That is, unless there's more here you want to do."

Roderick glanced back at the room with the grapes and baklava as if he had a hankering for one last bite. Then he wrapped his tunic around his waist and motioned toward the exit.

"Come on," he said. "We'll change into other clothes in the cars. We can catch up with Klara later."

There was some discussion about leaving Georgie's sister to her fate. But as Georgie tagged along in our wake, he assured us that she was a perennial attraction at these festivities and would be looked after with great diligence. So much for first impressions.

CHAPTER THIRTEEN

It was the old man who gave away Anton's refuge. I noticed him as soon as we entered the town square where I had first seen Anton. He was standing at the same cluster of tables where we'd sat and talked then. As before, we'd parked a distance away and walked into the pedestrian zone containing the cafes.

The old man and I spotted each other simultaneously. It was way too late for much to be going on. He was looking around as if that was what he was there to do. Our little group was hard to miss. The town was sufficiently far off the tourist track for foreigners to stand out from the crowd. Besides, he probably remembered us from our last visit.

"Look over to your left—as if you don't notice him," I told the others, "and head toward the far side of the square."

My sidelong squint to the right caught the back of the old man as he skirted tables and labored toward the shadows of an alley.

I turned to Georgie, whom I judged to be the best able of us to keep the old man in sight.

"Follow him quickly," I said, issuing a brief description of the fugitive. "We'll be right behind you."

Emilio, Diane and Greta obeyed like lambs. Roderick, of course, wanted to know what we were doing and why.

"I think the old man is a confidant of Anton," I told him as we strode after Georgie. "At any rate, he gave me that impression when I saw Anton here before."

There was no time to discuss further. Ahead of us Georgie

was already slaloming around chairs and about to tread the dark pavement of the alley slotted between the café and adjacent buildings.

Catching up with Georgie, we now had the old man well within sight. We could hear him panting as he climbed a flight of steps, his hands clutching at metal railings and head bowed as he pulled himself up.

"You better be right about this," Roderick whispered. "If the old geezer doesn't get a rest soon, we'll be had up for manslaughter."

Finally *the geezer* ascended to a porch and, without so much as knocking on the wooden expanse in front of him, pushed open the door and shuffled into a dimly lit hallway.

"Well, what do we do now?" Diane asked.

"We knock, and ask for Anton," said Greta, back to her cool-under-pressure normal self.

So that was what we did. More precisely, it was Greta who knocked. Then, when the old man at last peered around the door, she said, "We have come to see Anton." She said Anton quite forcefully, in case the old man's English wasn't up to the rest of the sentence.

"No Anton," he said with a shake of his head. Greta persisted.

"We think we saw our friend Anton go this way."

"No . . . no," the gatekeeper — for that's what he seemed to be — said firmly.

"We've come a long way to see him," Diane said. "We're just trying to help. If there's anything wrong . . ."

The old man was about to repeat his rebuff. Then, from out of the gloom behind him, came a voice we all recognized. Well, Greta, Diane, Roderick and I did anyway. Emilio might have done. Georgie most likely didn't.

"It's ok. Let them in."

The old man ushered us into the hall. Diane, first in, skirted around him, elbows tucked in and eyes averted.

"Nikolaos won't hurt you," came the voice from within, apparently anticipating her unease. "He's a family servant. Loyal and trustworthy."

At first the walls looked bare and rather grubby, but as my eyes adjusted to the dimness, I realized that the hall was strictly utilitarian and perhaps intended to give a rather down-at-heel impression to outsiders. Like the house exteriors and surroundings in this neighborhood—the hooded doorways and ubiquitous blue paint and twisting alleys—it was as if the whole idea was to conceal the lives of the residents. Only when one was admitted to the inner sanctums could one hope for candor, let alone intimacy.

The spacious room beyond the hall was a different matter entirely. Even with just the moon and table lamps, the high white walls and a polished tile floor seemed to revel in light. French doors opened on to a floodlit terrace and a garden, with a small pond and fountain visible in outline. Vases—amphorae, I think they call them—and plates were arranged on shelves and in niches, each one an upscale version of the rows we'd seen in the tourist shops, all etched with mythological beasts and warriors and such.

Anton stood in front of a sofa and beamed as we went in. At first his movements were tense and his facial muscles quivered with the strain of holding the smile. But as we greeted him with smiles of our own, he began to relax.

"It's great to see you, really it is," he began, embracing Greta first, then Diane and me, a bit more of a male bonding hug for Roderick, shaking hands with Emilio and wrapping up with an affectionate squeeze of Georgie's shoulder. Then a few words from Anton sent the old man to fetch assorted libations—wine, beer, the cloudy hard stuff that the locals consumed in great quantity, and lemonade for those of us who wanted to retain recall.

"You had us wondering," I said. "I mean, you seemed more concerned with getting away from us."

"I owe you an apology on that score," Anton said, to which there was a chorus from us about all the trouble we'd gone to tracking down the trio we thought were in peril, if not dead.

"It was very rude of me — after you'd come all this way," Anton sympathized. "God, what friends you are, to do that for us. It's all been a nightmare here, if you did but know."

"Well, here we are," Diane said as she sat in an armchair with a glass of wine. "Tell us about it."

Anton continued to pace in erratic zigzags.

"We, or rather I, have to be careful. Well, we all do really. It's not like back home where you know what's going on, even if you're in trouble. Here, you don't know who to trust. They could have a tail on you, even. Helen's trying to take care of it now, but . . ."

"Helen?" Emilio broke in. It was clear from the rising pitch in his voice that he'd been holding back on that subject. I mean, there we'd been, absorbed in what had happened to Anton, Klara and Reynard and barely a mention, I have to admit, about Helen.

"Yeah, I'll get to Helen in a minute," Anton promised. "God, where do I start?"

"Why not at the beginning," said Greta. By that time we'd taken possession of the seating opportunities afforded by the room, sipping at our various drinks and slumping into the cushions very much as you might expect people to after the night we'd had. To coin a cliché, none of us were as young as we used to be — except for Georgie for course, and in this context he didn't really count. Still, we were a receptive audience, and Anton didn't seem to need much encouragement. He spoke like a man who was dying to tell someone his story.

"I dunno. How far back do I go? Perhaps it seems a bit odd to you, the way Reynard, Klara, and I have hung out together all these years. I mean, I know we've all more or less kept in touch. But there's a lot that doesn't get revealed."

The wine I'd chosen was neither red nor white. A fortifying amber with an oily touch on the palette was the description that came to mind as I swirled it around in the glass. It went straight to my head, whatever the vintage, greatly enhancing the journey down Anton's memory lane. Indeed, I could have added detours that he didn't even mention. Telling detours they were, that could have revealed a lot.

For instance, I remembered a long weekend Reynard, Klara, Anton and I took in the west country. Reynard had rented a cottage, and it was as cozy as autumn retreats are intended to be. Confined by rain, we lounged in front of a log fire and passed around a spliff of ambrosial vegetative matter that Reynard had brought. He always acquired the best. It was an unspoken point of honor with him.

In retrospect, one of my greatest attributes is my ability to blend into the background. It's a talent you don't value much as a kid or even as a young adult, when being the life and soul of every gathering seems much more advantageous. Only with maturity does it dawn on you how much you can learn about people by being off their radar.

And so it was on that long ago occasion. Klara was at her most flirtatious, stripped down to a negligee—purple of course—and mouthing off in the BBC accent she reserved for moments of provocation.

The three of them were on a couch, with Reynard in an *I'm-in-command* pose in the middle. He had an arm over the shoulder of each of the others, applying enough pressure to encourage both of them to gradually fold in on him, like top-heavy bookends.

Before long Klara was nuzzling at belt level and Anton, though a little more brittle in his compliance, was not far above. From my pouffe next to the hearth, I watched Klara perform one of her celebrated party tricks — unzipping a fly without recourse to fingers — and fully anticipated that her encore would consist of an even more intimate demonstration.

Instead, she raised her head as if she'd suddenly had a better idea, which apparently she thought she had.

"Anton, it's your turn to do it," she said.

Even though that cottage was no lighter than our present surroundings, I could still make out the uncertainty in Anton's eyes. What we'd assumed up to that point — those of us who weren't directly involved — was that Anton was very much the passive partner in his relationship with Reynard. Reynard took the initiative, Anton complied. Did his reserve stem from fear of spiritual consequences, born of a strict moral upbringing? As far as we could tell, he thought the world of Reynard. It was just that the sex, and all the trimmings that go along with it, was definitely Dom/sub with those two. Later, as I've already explained, I got to understand Anton's motives better. But at the time, we put it down to guilt.

Anyway, this was quite a challenge Klara was issuing. Was Anton prepared to go down on his knees in front of Reynard's loins? It's one thing, as many a wife knows, to be done to and quite another to do. A different level of commitment entirely.

To sweeten the proposition, Klara put a hand on Anton's thigh. Even as she did so, there was an ambiguity about the gesture that left me, and perhaps Anton, wondering what purpose she intended to convey. As she well knew, no doubt.

"I'll do whatever you do," she said to him in a pillow-talk purr.

It was enough to goad Anton into action. Only when Reynard was squirming in anticipation did Klara's deception become clear. No doubt Anton would have seen the job through to completion, given that his understanding was that Klara would do the same to him. Oral bliss with Klara was, after all, everything he longed for.

What he wasn't prepared for was Klara nudging him aside to take his place. He watched in pained silence as trickles leaked out of the corners of Klara's still-pumping mouth and dribbled down into Reynard's pubic undergrowth.

"There you are," she said, as she rose with a giggle of triumph. "I did what you did. I didn't say to whom I'd do it."

It was episodes of this sort that made me think I had an idea where Anton was coming from when he started talking about the lot that hadn't got revealed. Klara's teasing was probably part of that lot. Being a plaything, bounced between Reynard and Klara, might have been rather exciting at first. But if went on year after year, surely it would get to anyone, even someone as placid as Anton.

Finally Anton had calmed down enough to sit on the edge of the sofa, and from this position he resumed his debriefing. We listened mostly in silence, with occasional utterances of surprise as we were brought up to date. Much of the back story was already known to some of us, of course.

"Tell us about the trip here and the boat you three supposedly chartered," an impatient Roderick demanded at one point. "Why didn't you three let us know what had happened? It would have saved us a rescue mission."

Anton disregarded the interruption. Perhaps he needed to recount all the details for his own mental health.

"When we came out here—on your ship, Emilio," he summed up, "I only knew part of what was going on. I suppose that was pretty typical of me, really. For years I'd been drifting along with what Reynard wanted, trying to match his concept of what I ought to be. We had our arguments and break-ups, but then I'd feel this emptiness after a while and get back in touch with him. I kept hoping that Klara would come to my rescue somehow."

"Is she here?" Emilio suddenly broke in. "Helen, I mean."

As I said, he was on a different wavelength from the rest of us.

"Er, well I'm coming to that," Anton said. "This *is* one of the family's properties. But, no, she's not here just at this moment . . . See, what I didn't know was that, before we even started out from England, Helen had confessed to Reynard all about her parents. I think she thought he would be upset about the parties and their whole lifestyle. Little did she know. Reynard must have just lapped it up. You can imagine him telling Klara, can't you. Castle orgies on a Mediterranean island? Next thing Helen knew, she was taking us back to what she thought she'd escaped from. It wasn't her scene at all."

Anton cleared his throat and took a gulp of his beverage while we all waited for more. None of his listeners, I'd venture to say, knew where he was headed with this account. Our breath was bated.

"Helen must have realized what her parents had in mind," he continued, his face creased as if deciding on the best way to explain. "I certainly didn't. I think Reynard probably went along with it, thinking it would be a bit of fun.

"At first I thought they, Helen's parents, had just taken a liking to me. But then it began to get odd. Helen's mother wanted me to go shopping with her. We'd drive from their home at the fortress, where we were all staying, to the port. Just the two of us. When we got there we'd call on that lady — you must have seen her when you arrived tonight. She was sort of doing the maître d' bit at the gate with her husband."

"The lady with the mermaid tattoo?" Greta asked.

"Yeah, that's the one. Anyway, they'd have a couple of glasses of wine and start giggling and cuddling up against each other, and they'd start ordering me around and wanting me to serve the drinks. Next I know I'm being told to get on my knees in front of them and, well you can probably guess what they wanted me to do.

"Well, that wasn't so bad. I mean anyone with a tongue can't go far wrong in that department, can they? Then they brought out the toys. Again, I don't mind witnessing a little artificially induced stimulation. Except the next thing was, they moved on to me. So there I was sucking the nail varnish off one pair of feet while a set of fingernails on the other side was prying my buttocks apart and pushing who knows what into me."

"Not exactly unknown territory for you though, was it?" Roderick butted in with slick sarcasm.

"Okay, point taken," Anton acknowledged. "Not exactly torture, I'll agree. Well, torture of a type, but I wasn't protesting too hard . . . But then Helen's father got in on the act. He was a well-built fellow, all muscles and gruff voice."

"Was?" I asked, picking up on the tense.

"Was. Yeah. I'll get to that. Things with Helen's mother really began to get out of hand. I told Reynard and Klara about it, but they just acted like it was a joke. Perhaps they even were in on the joke. I don't know."

"Sounds like Helen's father got in on it anyway," Roderick interrupted. "Judging from what I heard. Actually that maître d' lady you mentioned, her and her husband were telling me."

"They would," Anton continued. "As I said, she and Helen's mother were pretty tight. Anyway, one night Helen's father found his wife and me . . . well, she'd tied me over the back of a sofa. Little bit of innocent bondage. I could go along with that. Next I knew he'd decided I was getting too friendly with his wife and was threatening punishment."

"Gave you a spanking?" Roderick suggested with a grin.

"Humiliating, it was," Anton said.

"Seem to remember Reynard trying that on you once or twice," Roderick said.

"Well, only when Klara was around," Anton replied. "It was sort of a game. I quite enjoyed it when she was involved. Doctor and nurse and all that . . . But this was different. I mean I hardly knew the man. It's one thing being teasingly admonished by a soft and sympathetic hand. It's quite another to be walloped by a bruiser like him."

"Did you tell Reynard and Klara?" Diane asked. She'd been quietly sipping in words and wine with the concentration of a fellow traveler who knew what it was like to be subject to command.

"Yeah, but they said I should go along with it, that we were guests and we owed them on that account. So it just escalated. Soon they — Helen's parents that is — wanted me there when they had sex. Not just them either, but that other couple, with the tattoos. The four of them would expect me to clean them up afterward, and I don't mean with a towel."

Emilio grimaced.

"Did Helen know?" he asked.

I had the feeling that if her parents had been mating with dolphins, the only question on Emilio's mind would be what effect it had on Helen.

"Not the details," Anton replied. "But she had her suspicions. It certainly cooled her feelings for Reynard, that he'd let it happen, encouraged it really. I didn't tell her what was going on, of course. But she'd been uncomfortable with her parents' activities for quite a while, what with the parties and what not. So we kinda drifted together in mutual support."

Through the French windows I could see that dawn was not far off. The courtyard was shapeshifting with the intensifying luster. Foliage and walls were revealing their true forms. The vagaries of night were being breached.

For a minute or two there was a lull in the room. How we'd lasted the night without sleep I don't know. The naps most of us took the previous afternoon must have helped — that, and the ebb and flow of adrenalin.

Then, from somewhere else in the house, the jangle of a telephone cut through the silence. The old man reappeared and beckoned.

"Excuse me a minute," Anton said as he left the room. We strained to hear, at least I did. But his voice was muffled, and even when he talked with the old man, it wasn't clear what was being said. I could hear references to *she,* but which *she* I wasn't sure. All I *could* say was that there was an urgency to it. Finally Anton returned.

"Is it Helen?" Emilio asked in a tense voice. "Is she all right?"

"She was supposed to drive back to the fortress," Anton said. "A few things she had to take care of. Driving Georgie's sister back to the hotel, for one. That was Mrs. Mermaid, as you call her, on the phone. Helen hasn't shown up. They're a bit pissed about it, actually. Georgie's sister is still waiting for a lift home."

"Shouldn't we go look for her?" Emilio persisted. "Where would she be?"

"Well, I'm wondering . . ." Anton sounded dubious about revealing more until a decisive question pressed him on it.

"Yes?"

It was Greta's turn to be inquisitor.

"It's the boat, you see," Anton continued rather hesitantly. "I hadn't got to that part yet. But I think she's gone to the bay where the boat is. It's still moored out there. Supposedly it's being held by the police while they complete their inquiries. Who knows where those will go, though?"

"So she's gone to take a look at it?" Roderick asked. "If she can find it, she's doing better than we did . . . Maybe we were looking in the wrong bay."

"A bit more than just taking a look I think," Anton said, glossing over Roderick's implied inquiry. "Perhaps I better get out there."

"Well, not without us," Roderick told him. "Come on, the cars aren't far. Let's get going."

CHAPTER FOURTEEN

We strode with varying effort back the way we had come. Past the now-deserted café tables and across the square we went, with Anton peering up at clouds tossed like spume by a rising wind.

"I don't like the look of the sky at all," he said amid the huffs and puffs of our straining party.

Dawn was more than a suggestion by the time we reached the bay. A frieze of dark bulbous ectoplasm floated across the faint pink of a new day.

How Roderick, Greta, and Diane had missed the boat on their previous expedition to the bay seemed hard to explain. There it was bobbing in the surf just beyond a jetty. But perhaps, as Roderick protested, it had been moved there after their reconnaissance.

"The police still have the whole affair in tow, as it were," Anton said. "So it could be you're right."

The patio of a bar gave us shelter. There was no one around, and so we unstacked chairs and stared out at breakers smashing against rock while we considered further where Helen might be.

"You still haven't told us how the boat fits into all this," Roderick said.

"Yeah," Diane added, "weren't there supposed to be bodies? We thought you'd been drowned."

Anton's face puckered, and I took it as a sign he was weighing his response, as well he might. After all, we'd come a long way and taken a lot of trouble on his behalf.

"It was a day like this," Anton said after hesitation. "Actually, at first it wasn't. It started off calm and beautiful, and so Helen's parents decided they wanted to go sailing in their boat and that I had to go with them."

"That's *their* boat out there?" Greta asked. Prompted by a nod from Anton, we exchanged wide-eyed expressions and exclamations as we digested the information. "That accounts for why we couldn't work out where it was rented from," Roderick said. "So what did they want you along for . . . or is that a sore spot, so to speak?"

Even at his most serious, Roderick couldn't resist a pun.

"Well may you ask," Anton continued, zipping his jacket and raising his voice to be heard over the effects of the wind. Everything not secured was rattling or banging or squeaking—a table on an uneven surface, a window shutter with a faulty latch, a sign swinging on a chain. It was most distracting. Georgie, with the initiative of an experienced hotel hand, had found kindling and started a fire in a brazier behind a wall.

"I didn't want to go," Anton went on as we huddled around the flames—more for comfort than a need for warmth. "I knew what would happen. Once we got away from the harbor they stripped off, and of course they wanted me to do the same.

"After a while they pulled down the sails, or whatever the term is, and they dropped anchor. Then it was a case of my having to satisfy every whim they had. Serve food, some of which was rather intimately placed. Clean them up, in ways I'll leave to your imagination. All the time, they were drinking and giggling and smoking dope, and I was expected to join in. It went on like this for hours, and if they felt I wasn't serving them properly then there'd be a playful little smack across my backside. For a time I was chained and handcuffed. Helen's mother sort of tricked me into it. I had to agree to various demands before they let me go. I just had enough. I had this feeling they were setting me up for something—"

"Like what?" Diane interrupted.

"I dunno," Anton said with a shrug. "You never knew with those two, what extremes they'd go to. Anyway, resentment had been building in me for a while, between them and Reynard and Klara. I suppose I have a problem with asserting myself sometimes. Letting things happen to you can be exhilarating; it can be a rush. But there's a price to be paid, for sure.

"Helen's parents went snorkeling. It was late in the afternoon, and I was so upset that, on the spur of the moment, I thought *what if the boat drifted away from them.* Would serve them right. I wasn't thinking too clearly, what with the drinking and smoking.

"There were some fishing boats passing by. We'd waved at them earlier, so I had to wait until they'd gone away. Then I hauled up the anchor—I'd watched her parents use a winch to lower it.

"Before I knew it the boat had gone much further than I expected. Suddenly the wind had come up and the sea was getting quite choppy. I couldn't see Helen's parents any more. Dusk was coming on, too.

"I suppose I panicked a bit. I tried to lower the anchor, but perhaps it was too deep where I'd drifted to, because the anchor wouldn't grip. The boat was being blown toward the shore and finally it was near enough that I made up my mind to swim for it. In my mind was the vision of that boat being swept away and me being lost at sea. Better take my chance while I could, I thought.

"I was near exhaustion by the time I dragged myself up on the shingle. Behind me I could see the waves being whipped up and those anvil-type clouds coming in behind them. What was I to do? Somewhere out there were Helen's parents, but there was little I could do to help them. It was all I could do to lie there shivering. My legs and arms were so numb I no longer had any control over them. Eventually a fisherman or someone of that sort found me, and he must have got word to Helen. She's been the one person in all this who's really supported me."

Roderick looked doubtful.

"Wasn't she upset about her parents?" he asked.

"Of course," Anton agreed. "But she knew what they'd been putting me through. I mean, there's been a strain in that relationship for quite a while . . . Actually I haven't told her everything that happened yet. I need to face up to it, I know."

As Anton talked, I noticed that Greta was paying more attention to the sea than the rest of us. The two masts of the boat were swaying, and at times they were all that could be seen above the whitecaps. She was leaning over the wall, still wearing the turquoise dress from the party—although she had added a shawl that had been in one of the cars. Suddenly her body stiffened and her focus seemed drawn to one spot.

It may be inappropriate to mention how elegant she looked poised there. The oblique light from the direction of the sea accentuated her hair and her dress was virtually airbrushed on to her breasts and behind. She was a picture from a magazine fashion spread—and all the more captivating for being unaware of it. Funny how mistimed such observations can be.

"There's someone out there," she said. We gathered close to her, as if we might thereby see through her eyes.

"It's a dinghy," Roderick added.

Reactions among us ranged from curiosity to alarm, with Emilio being the most animated.

"It's her," he all but shouted. "What's she doing?"

"Trying to reach the boat, by the look of it," Anton said.

"She'll never make it," Diane said. "Look at those waves. That little dinghy will overturn."

The dread of it was enough to send Emilio sprinting

toward the jetty. Anton was in his tracks, and the rest of us gaped for a minute before jogging after them.

"This is madness," Diane said. "We need to get police or lifeboat men or someone with equipment."

"There's no time," Roderick blurted in the midst of panting. Jogging was clearly not his usual pursuit. "Whatever needs to be done has to be done now, or she's lost."

Emilio seemed little more than a stick figure ahead of us, filtered as he was by the squall. Neither wind nor water held him, however, as he bounded along the jetty. Anton was close behind, and every few seconds—seconds that felt like hours—the dinghy would bob out of a trough, with Helen— now confirmed by Emilio's cries as the rower—struggling to keep the oar blades from being sucked under.

For an instant Emilio stood on the jetty's edge, bent over, yelling at Helen by the look of it. Spray almost consumed him from the waist down.

"Oh god," Diane gasped. "It's going to flip, isn't it?"

Sure enough, the dinghy lurched in the clasp of a breaker. And then it tipped completely. All that could be seen of it was an upturned hull. Its lone occupant had vanished.

To give him credit, Emilio jumped into the surf without hesitation. For a second I could see his head above the water and his arms striking the surface as he battled toward the dinghy. A second later he'd be out of sight, and then a second more and I'd catch another glimpse.

Anton had found a rope and was on his knees, trying to arrange it in a serviceable loop. Task accomplished, he balanced as far out on the jetty as he could, clearly waiting for the right moment to hurl the coils gathered in his arms.

The waiting was agony. It was like watching a car accident or some terrifying drama in a theater, and feeling helpless. We could have run along the jetty and backed up Anton, I suppose. Instead we just gawked as if we'd been turned to stone.

Eventually Anton hurled the loop end of the rope. Into the midst of the waves it went. We had to imagine desperate hands grasping at it. So fierce had the sea become that nothing of Emilio or Helen could be seen. Then the rope was taut and Anton began leaning back and tugging. He was not a brawny man, as I've already explained, and it finally dawned on us that rescue was in the balance.

"Come on," Roderick bellowed. "Let's get over there."

It must have looked like a tug of war team—not that anyone was making comparisons at the time. We were hauling on that rope as if lives depended on it, which of course they did. Our feet slipped on the slick stone of the jetty, the rope seared our hands, and more than one of us must have nursed scrapes and bruises in the aftermath.

I was faintly aware of arms gripping the loop out there in the water, and then Anton had let go of the rope and was rushing forward to clamp on to those arms and haul for all he was worth. In a minute there was Helen sprawled on the cold stone like the carcass of a fish. Limp and sodden as she was, she looked beyond help.

But then Greta began giving first aid. Trust Greta, God bless her, to know what to do.

"Where's Emilio?" Roderick said in a tone of genuine alarm rare for him.

We scanned the sea, focusing on the upturned hull which the cresting waves were swiftly bearing away from us. Some of us even yelled his name, although looking back on it that wasn't going to do much good. It wasn't as if he'd be swimming off in the wrong direction. Well, maybe he would. Those troughs were awfully deep, and the fact was we never saw head nor hand of him again. Not till a day or so later anyway, when his body drifted into a harbor just along the coast. Even then, I didn't actually see him. Didn't have the stomach for it. I think it was Helen or Anton who identified him for the authorities.

After a minute — another of those measures of time which don't seem big enough to pack in all the anguish we felt — Helen began to cough. Out of her mouth came a geyser of water. Then more spluttering. Anton gently shifted her into a sitting position and crouched with his arm around her shoulders.

"How are you feeling?" we asked, and a few more stupid questions. But what *do* you say in those circumstances? Something, anything to show your concern. It doesn't matter what really.

CHAPTER FIFTEEN

Georgie's sister had a name. We knew that she must have had one, of course. But after days of calling her "Georgie's sister" we'd relegated her to her brother's appendage. Unforgivable really, but she'd seemed such a retiring sort that we'd slipped into thinking of her in terms of her relationship rather than as a person in her own right.

"I'm Selene," she said with a ready handshake for each of us as we passed through the hotel lobby on our way to breakfast. "You remember me?"

Well, of course we did. Visions of the party at Helen's family fortress would not soon fade. Hard to forget her delectable bottom bent over like a couple of eager mushrooms ripe for the picking.

This seemed a different girl, though, from the one I had watched spread-eagled while strangers amused themselves with her intimate parts. Her forthright greeting was not what we anticipated from the shy receptionist who had observed our initial arrival from behind the hotel counter.

That waist-length hair of hers still shimmered and there was still a slim grace to the way she moved, as if a sudden gust might cause levitation. But the confidence in the eyes hadn't been there before, and neither had the lip gloss that framed that captivating smile.

"Your sister is very perky this morning," I said to Georgie when he brought our coffee. We started slurping at the cups before he had a chance to reply. After spending the previous days recovering from Helen's rescue, we were just beginning

144

to feel we were ready for normal life again. That caffeine was overdue.

Georgie blushed a little as he replied.

"She's like that when she comes back from that place."

"You mean Helen's fortress?" Roderick asked, back to his blunt self now that we'd all had a chance to resume our normal personalities.

"Yes."

Apparently the topic was one Georgie felt a bit bashful about pursuing. Not so Roderick, who responded to Selene's perkiness in kind.

"Look at that derriere," he said as the brother hurried off with our breakfast orders. We squinted diplomatically in the direction of Selene sashaying over the polished wood of a small dance floor in the corner of the room — an area that came into its own, so we were told, when the locals were feeling frisky. At that moment however, its prime attraction was Selene's red satin pencil skirt straining to retain its contents.

"Wouldn't mind a few whirls with her," Roderick went on. "Funny how she's changed, isn't it? All that bondage the other night must have been liberating for her. I wonder if it works that way sometimes."

The pause that followed was an obvious invitation for comment, but none came, and Roderick was obliged to probe further.

"I mean, if you look at it a certain way, there's something rather exhilarating and fulfilling about it," he continued. "Being the center of attention, for one thing, and all those people venting their inner desires on you. It's self-sacrifice at its most altruistic. Spiritual, you might say."

Even those of us close to Roderick tend to fall for the bait when his tongue gets wedged that far into his cheek. He'll just keep saying things till he touches a nerve.

"Depends on a person's state of mind," Diane said, no

doubt drawing on her experience of submitting to Klara's whims. "I mean it can be a high, if the vibes are right, but it can also grow to be pretty demoralizing . . . Just ask Anton."

The observation was clearly addressed to the man in question, who was just then walking up to our table with an arm around Helen's shoulder in a proud and protective clasp. Actually it took me a few seconds to realize who she was. I'd only had fleeting glimpses of her in the car park at the fortress, and it would hardly be fair to judge her on her near-drowned state when we were on the jetty.

"Ask me what?" Anton asked. Then, on being given more information, he said, "I can only speak for myself. With Reynard and me, it just went on too long."

"Well, looks like you've been freed from that now," was Roderick's conclusion.

Helen was caressing Anton's arm and shoulder and smiling at him as if each word he said came straight from Delphi. Now that she was on the mend from her dip in the ocean, I could understand why she had held such sway over the late lamented Emilio as well as Anton.

Even in the wake of a near-death experience, there were shades of that immaculate bearing that young women accustomed to privilege sometimes have. Granted, she'd spent a couple of hours that morning being restored to perfection at a beauty salon. But it showed. Everything from her hair to her figure, from her clothes to the glow of her skin looked to be the work of experts in their fields. Once I got to know her a bit better, though, I discovered that she was all heart beneath it. Poise can so easily be mistaken for arrogance.

"Helen and I are going back to England," Anton said in an offhand way, as if he didn't want to make a big issue out of it. The news was not a total surprise in view of the obvious affection between the two, but we still craved for details.

"Well, that's wonderful," Greta said, and as usual she

meant it.

"Yeah," Anton continued. "Um, there are a few things to clear up first."

"Like your parents, Helen," Roderick said. He wasn't being hostile, just voicing what the rest of us were thinking probably. "I mean, aren't there inquiries or something about what happened to them?"

"Sorry," said Helen in a resonant voice. "My English is not good yet. I take care . . ."

Fluency, or rather lack of it, didn't seem to interfere with her self-confidence. Still, Anton came to her rescue. Apparently they were getting accustomed to helping each other out.

"Helen's been tremendous," he said, "considering the stress of this whole thing. The family has a lot of influence here, so she's managed to keep it all pretty quiet. Now she just wants to get away and forget about it."

"So what about Reynard and Klara?" Diane asked.

"They're going to stay and look after the fortress for a while," Anton replied.

"That should be right up their street," Roderick said. "What with old Seahorse and Mrs. Mermaid in the neighborhood, they should manage to keep the festivities buzzing along."

With a nod and a faint smile, Anton acknowledged as much.

"They seem to feel that way too."

It's amazing how quickly a place can feel like home. Even the people that come with it can seem like old friends before you know it.

Our final night at the hotel was subdued. I, for one, was thinking about how I'd probably never be there again, and I expect Roderick, Diane, and Greta had similar preoccupations. There wasn't really much to pack. Our suitcases were supplemented by a few souvenirs we'd picked up in the port. Roderick had bought a fairly sizeable statue of Poseidon. Or was it Zeus? Anyway, it looked like it might pose a problem at the check-in counter when we finally reached the airport. But when it came to it, they just waved us through, and Roderick propped the immortal one, swathed in protective polythene, against an empty seat on the plane. Apparently gods still get special treatment in that part of the world.

While we were packing, Anton dropped by to wish us a safe trip. Helen's aversion to flying hadn't subsided, so they were returning by sea—actually by the same cruise ship on which Emilio had served, which seemed like it might feel a little weird. She couldn't be blamed, of course, for his fate. Neither could she help it if he was besotted with her. Like a lot of us, he just didn't know when it was over.

Diane, incidentally, had been persuaded to take the plane on a "once only" basis. A heavy dose of pharmaceuticals would see her through. After all, we pointed out, little pills used to get us through all kinds of situations and that was without even leaving the ground, physically at least.

"I still don't get what Helen was doing in that dinghy," Roderick said.

"She was doing it for m,e really," Anton told him. "She was terrified the police would find some evidence that I'd been on the boat when her parents had drowned. We were getting close to each other by then, and she didn't want me involved. That, of course, and all the sex aid stuff that was aboard. I think maybe she thought . . . Well, actually I don't know what she thinks . . ."

"The police might think it looks a bit dicey," Roderick conceded, "what with you pulling up the anchor and drifting off like that."

"Yeah, although I haven't yet explained that to Helen quite as fully as I should," Anton went on. "So Helen's first notion was to avoid a big scandal. A couple of foreigners up to hi-jinks on a borrowed boat seemed like a good cover story. With all due respect to Reynard and Klara, their deaths wouldn't have the same impact locally as Helen's parents' would have. Call it identity confusion. Protecting the family's reputation counts for a lot around here."

We watched Anton strut off with Helen at his side.

"He's changed, don't you think?" Roderick observed. "Firmer step. More sure of himself . . . Love will do that, I suppose. In a way, it seems like he's leaving the old Anton behind."

"Along with the old Helen perhaps," I suggested.

"It's turned out well if that's the case," concluded Roderick, seemingly determined to end with some philosophy. "The shadow of death brought us here, and we leave in the light of transformation."

It was a wrench, the next morning, saying goodbye to Georgie and Selene.

"We see you again someday," Selene said, beaming and embracing as if she were Mrs. Mermaid herself.

"So, just to be sure," I said to Georgie. "Our two other friends. Lord Goat and the lady with the purple nails? That was them at the party?"

I did an impression of a man standing with arms folded while a woman gyrated at his side. Georgie caught on with a grin and nodded.

We'd already decided not to try to track down Reynard and Klara at the fortress. It may seem a strange decision, after going all that way to find out what had happened to them. But we *had* found out, and Greta had expressed it for all of us when she said, "Let's leave it the way we imagine them best."

"That's right," Roderick agreed. "No anticlimax. That's never a good thing to remember someone by."

In my mind, Reynard and Klara were already immortals. I wanted to preserve those first impressions. Reynard's intuitive grasp of a person's inhibitions and how to free them. Klara's iconic allure. How much more stimulating to honor the myths without the aftermath. Impact enough for a lifetime. No need to update.

"And it's not as if we'll never hear from them again," Diane added.

How right she was. In fact, about the first thing I saw when I got home was a very dated postcard with one of those now familiar sun-drenched bays on the front of it.

"Don't believe all you hear," Reynard had written. "It's greatly exaggerated. Why don't you come visit?"

YOU MAY ALSO ENJOY THE FOLLOWING FROM EXTASY BOOKS INC:

Rules Are Meant to be Broken
KL Wilde

Excerpt

"You're breaking the law in that dress," he said, instantly regretting it. It was a terrible line. Most certainly the worst he'd ever uttered, possibly in the history of the English language.

Every man in the crowded bar had probably tried his luck on the woman in the red dress. She sat alone at a corner table, straight backed and exuding confidence. Her crimson outfit hugged every curve. Combined with her raven hair and black rimmed glasses, it only served to highlight her flawless ivory skin.

The slightest crease invaded the corner of her wonderfully curved mouth. The gaze of her green eyes swept over him, assessing him from bootstraps to hair gel. He could only hope she hadn't noticed the quality of his opening gambit.

"That's a hideous pickup line," she drawled.

So much for hope. He winced. "It was, wasn't it?"

A large, sweaty man bumped into him, carrying four precariously balanced drinks. He stepped aside, waving the man through, before returning to the woman in red

Bowing, he added, "Sorry, I shouldn't have disturbed you. You deserve a much better line than that. You deserve no line at all. I should have approached you genuinely, and I'm only just realising that, and now, I'm officially babbling. I'll go and let you get on with your life. Have a nice night and, ah, life. Sorry about, you know, being a creep."

Who is this guy? Stripped of his usual easy confidence, he had devolved into a babbling mess. Perhaps recent events had affected him far worse than he'd realised. Maybe it was the unfamiliar location. Maybe it was the vision in front of him. Her level of self-assuredness was intimidating, but he'd managed to converse with far less approachable women before. Tonight wasn't his night. He was off his game. Maybe just this once, he'd be better to cut his losses and head back to the hotel.

Recent advice from his mates back home in Australia had been to get back on the horse as soon as possible. He'd reluctantly agreed with them to try, though his heart wasn't in it. They'd accused him of being a serial monogamist—a fate usually reserved for nerds with small dicks, if they were to be believed. Despite his protests, maybe they were right. The dismal failure of his usually flawless technique demonstrated that perhaps he'd rushed back into the saddle too soon.

Before him, the woman in red waved an elegant hand. It lacked an overall direction, so he didn't know whether it was dismissive or if she wanted him closer to give him a piece of her mind.

Instinct told him to leave, but he wanted to remain close to this goddess, if only for a moment longer. Her face could be considered angelic, but even from their limited interaction, he could see a hint of mischief in her eyes. They were incredibly expressive, providing a tantalising glimpse as to what lay below the alluring surface.

Her face and body were not to be easily forgotten, and remaining in her presence gave him the chance to commit every feature, every curvature to memory. He'd use the memory later when he inevitably retired to his hotel room alone.

Loud shouts emanated from the doorway as friends greeted each other. A rush of frigid air rushed in from the freezing New York night. Coats were shed and greetings exchanged.

The woman in red crinkled her nose. "A man whose vocabulary is bigger than his muscles. How unusual." Her gaze darted to his bicep, and he flexed instinctively to ensure it was hard as a rock. "Did you get a physique like that from wrestling crocodiles and deadly snakes Down Under?"

She was good at picking up accents. "Not quite. I'm a professional lifesaver."

"Lifesaver?"

"Oh, that's right you guys call it something different. Uh, lifeguard. On the beach. Like on Baywatch."

She nodded. "I could use one of those."

Arching her back, she wriggled in her chair, a move that emphasised the full force of her sizable breasts. If she noticed his sharp intake of breath, she didn't acknowledge it. Using her red high-heeled shoe, she slowly pushed out the chair in front of her. Her focus darted from the chair to him rocking on his heels and back again in a well-crafted, arching and challenging eyebrow.

He liked challenges. He'd once been accused of never backing down from one. This definitely wasn't the time to start.

He was thankful for the offer to sit. He didn't fancy standing in the middle of the bar on his own. Despite the three beers he'd already drunk, his mouth was as dry as his grandfather's toolbox. The room was oppressively hot, but sitting before this woman, he felt oddly cool. For the first time since this horrific week began, he forgot the raised voices and slammed doors and remembered how to smile.

As he offered his thanks to the woman in red, she held up her hand. "Oh, don't think you're getting anywhere. I'm just bored."

"I can't see how. I assume you've had your hands full

fending off this lot," he said, motioning to the packed room of far more men than women, the mood jovial. Drinks cascaded over the front bar served by the lone barman.

"You'd think so, right? No, you and your sad little line were the first sniff of conversation I've had all night. Not a nibble, and I do love a chat. Well, I say that, but I've already formed a deep and profound relationship with the barman."

He looked at the harried man furiously pouring cocktails. The barman's hair was like something out of a boy-band film clip, and his well-moisturised cheekbones were baby-bottom smooth and fake-tanned.

When a similarly well-groomed man swanned in, the barman yelled, "Hey, girl!" and the two exchanged air kisses.

He snorted and turned to the woman in red. "I'm sure the two of you will be very happy together. Though you should probably warn your parents that grandkids will be off the cards."

"Mitsy and I will be very happy together. Thank you, Mr. Cynical." She couldn't mask her smirk that time.

His cheeks stretched into a full smile for the first time in days. She had a wicked sense of humour, too. Damn. Beautiful, funny, and smart. Tonight wasn't the time to be off his game. If he was going to get back on a horse, God, let it be this one, even if he wasn't a hundred percent sure of his jockey skills anymore.

The reverberation of Beth's rejection still rung in his ears. How had he not seen it coming? Was he that clueless about women? Yet here he was less than seventy-two hours later, already considering another one. He gave his head a slight shake. Picking apart his past relationships could wait.

He'd picked this woman because he needed to let off some steam. She definitely radiated steam, though she'd also proven to be more than just a gorgeous face worthy of a free drink. She had charm. She also knew how to push his buttons. A lethal combination.

He shrugged. "Well, if none of these other fellas have the

courage to talk to you, then you've chosen a bar full of idiots."

"Careful there, surfer-dude. Don't make me like you."

"Sorry," he said.

"That's better."

Extending his hand, he offered, "Hi, I'm Xavier."

She paused before her delicate fingers reached out and curled around his. It was a timid handshake. Not what he expected from such a confident woman, but her hand held his for a fraction longer than the social norm. She gave no verbal reply.

"Do you have a name?" he prompted.

"Several. They come in handy when filling in forms, ordering at Starbucks, and so forth."

"Are you always this mysterious?"

Hesitating, she replied, "Not normally, no."

For the first time he saw a slight fracture in her confidence in the hint of a self-deprecating smile. Was this all an act? Was the stunning vision before him not quite what she seemed?

Regardless, he was well on his way to smitten. Even if she wasn't as self-assured as she'd like to appear, he couldn't deny he was intrigued by this whip-smart, beautiful woman.

Into the silence, she asked, "I assume from your accent, you're here to audition for the next Thor movie?"

He mocked a frown. "Not every Australian is related to Chris Hemsworth, you know."

The corners of her mouth turned down slightly, and she quickly took a sip of her drink, maybe to cover the cheeky grin.

"You're playing with me, aren't you?"

Crossing her legs slowly, she asked, "What's wrong with playing?" As she did, the tip of her shoe brushed the inside of his leg. Her words, slow and deliberate, and her tilted head told him it was no accident. The game had officially changed. He sat up straighter. He didn't know the rules, but he definitely wanted to be a player.

"I see. Your accent, it's not from New York, is it? North-

Eastern maybe?"

"Not bad." She gave a slight bow.

"I'm guessing you're a visitor like me. Or is this place a usual haunt?"

"First time," she said, still smiling. "I don't get out much usually. I had to sneak—" She snapped her mouth shut as if she'd said too much.

"Sneak? Makes it sound like you tied your bedsheets together and climbed down the side of a building."

"Something like that."

"So, with the accent, I'm going to take a stab and say—"

The ice-queen persona returned with the raise of an imperious brow. "No, we're done with that conversation. Try something else. You were doing so well there for a minute."

ABOUT THE AUTHOR

A.L. Means grew up in the UK and now lives in Phoenix, Arizona. He has authored fiction and nonfiction in various genres, using different pen names, and has spent much of his working life as a journalist.

His fiction includes a self-published novel entitled Shine Like The Sun and two light-hearted tales suitable for readers of most ages, The Trouble Upstream and When Rabbits Ran Rampant.

As Andrew Means, he has written biographies of novelist and essayist George Orwell and the rock group Pink Floyd as well as Some Memories, a memoir about the childhood of the late Country-Western singer Marty Robbins, who lived in the Phoenix area before and after World War Two.

www.ingramcontent.com/pod-product-compliance
Lightning Source LLC
Chambersburg PA
CBHW060825120626
46557CB00001B/367